MARIE FERRARELLA

Colton by Marriage

D1044613

ROMANTIC
SUSPENSE

Special thanks and acknowledgment to Marie Ferrarella for her contribution to the Coltons of Montana miniseries.

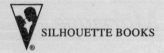

SILHOUETTE BOOKS

Recycling programs for this product may not exist in your area.

ISBN-13: 978-0-373-27686-8

COLTON BY MARRIAGE

Books by Marie Ferrarella

Silhouette Romantic Suspense

*Cavanaugh Justice
**Capturing the Crown
‡The Doctors Pulaski
‡‡Mission: Impassioned

MARIE FERRARELLA

This *USA TODAY* bestselling and RITA® Award-winning author has written almost two hundred books for Silhouette and Harlequin, some under the name of Marie Nicole. Her romances are beloved by fans worldwide. Visit her Web site at www.marieferrarella.com.

To
Bonnie G. Smith.
Thank you for
having
such a wonderful daughter.

Prologue

"It's here, Sheriff." Unable to contain his excitement, Boyd Arnold all but hopped up and down as he pointed toward the murky body of water. "I saw it right here, in the creek, when Blackie ran into the water and I chased him out."

Blackie was what Boyd called his black Labrador retriever. Naming the dog Blackie had been the only unimaginative thing Boyd had ever done. Aside from that one example of dullness, the small-time rancher had an incredibly healthy imagination.

Some people claimed that it was a mite *too* healthy. At one time or another, Boyd had sworn he'd seen a ghost crossing his field, watched in awe as a UFO landed near Honey Creek, the body of water that the town had been named after, and now he was claiming to have seen a dead body in that very same creek.

As the town's recently elected sheriff, thirty-three-year-old Wes Colton would have liked just to have dismissed Boyd's newest tall tale as another figment of the man's overworked imagination. But, *because* he was the recently elected sheriff of Honey Creek, he couldn't. He was too new at the job to point to a gut feeling about things and so he was legally bound to check out each and every story involving wrongdoing no matter how improbable or wild it sounded.

Dead bodies were not the norm in Honey Creek. Most likely someone had dumped a mannequin in the creek in order to play a trick on the gullible Boyd. He hadn't put a name to the so-called body when he'd come running into the office earlier, tripping over his tongue as if it had grown to three times its size as he tried to say what it was he saw.

"Was it a woman, Boyd?" Wes asked now, trying to find the humor in the situation, although, he had to admit, between the heat and the humidity, his sense of humor was in extremely short supply today. Local opinion had it that a woman of the inflatable variety would be the only way Boyd would be able to find any female companionship at all.

Wes would have much rather been in his air-conditioned office, going over paperwork—something he usually disliked and a lot of which the last sheriff had left as payback for Wes winning the post away from him—than facing the prospect of walking through the water searching for a nonexistent body.

"I think it was a man. Tell the truth, Sheriff, I didn't stick around long enough to find out. Never can tell when you might come across one of them zombie types, or those body-snatchers, you know."

Wes looked at him. Boyd's eyes were all but bulging out. The man was actually serious. He shook his head. "Boyd, you want my advice? You've got to stop renting those old horror movies. You've got a vivid enough imagination as it is."

"This wasn't my imagination, Sheriff," Boyd insisted stubbornly with feeling. "This was a real live dead person."

Wes didn't bother pointing out the blatant contradiction in terms. Instead, he stood at the edge of the creek and looked around.

There was nothing but the sound of mosquitoes settling in for an afternoon feed.

A lot of mosquitoes, judging by the sound of it.

It was going to be a miserable summer, Wes thought. Just as he began to turn toward Boyd to tell the rancher that he must have been mistaken about the location of this "body," something caught Wes's eye.

Flies.

An inordinate number of flies.

Mosquitoes weren't making that noise, it was flies.

Flies tended to swarm around rotting meat and waste. Most likely it was the latter, but Wes had a strong feeling that he wasn't going to be free of Boyd until he at least checked out what the insects were swarming around.

"There, Sheriff, look there," Boyd cried excitedly, pointing to something that appeared to be three-quarters submerged in the creek.

Something that had attracted the huge number of flies.

There was no way around not getting his newly cleaned uniform dirty, Wes thought. Resigning himself to the unpleasant ordeal, Honey Creek's newly minted sheriff waded in.

Annoyance vanished as he drew closer to what the flies were laying claim to.

"Damn, but I think you're right, Boyd. That *does* look like a body," Wes declared. Forgetting about his uniform, he went in deeper. Whatever it was was only a few feet away.

"See, I told you!" Boyd crowed, happy to be vindicated. He was grinning from ear to ear like a little kid on Christmas morning. His expression was in sharp contrast to the sheriff's. The latter had become deadly serious.

It appeared to be a dead body all right. Did it belong to some vagrant who'd been passing through when he'd arbitrarily picked Honey Creek to die?

Or had someone dumped a body here from one of the neighboring towns? And if so, which one?

Bracing himself, Wes turned the body over so that he could view the face before he dragged the corpse out.

When he flipped the dead man over, his breath stopped in his lungs. The man had a single bullet in the middle of his forehead and he was missing half his face.

But the other half could still be made out.

At the same moment, unable to stay back, Boyd peered over his shoulder. The rancher's eyes grew huge and he cried out, "It's Mark Walsh!" No sooner was the name out of his mouth than questions and contradictions occurred to Boyd. "But he's dead." Confused, Boyd stared at Wes, waiting for him to say something that made sense out of this. "How can he look that fresh? He's been dead fifteen years!"

"Apparently Walsh wasn't as dead as we thought he was," Wes told him.

It was extremely difficult for Wes to maintain his decorum, not to mention an even voice, when all he could think of was that finally, after all these years, his brother was going to get out of jail.

Because Damien Colton had been convicted of a murder that had never happened.

Until now.

Chapter 1

Duke Colton didn't know what made him look in that direction, but once he did, he couldn't look away. Even though he wanted to.

Moreover, he wanted to keep walking. To pretend that he hadn't seen her, especially not like that.

Susan Kelley's head was still down, her short, dark-blond hair almost acting like a curtain, and she seemed oblivious to the world around her as she sat on the bench to the side of the hospital entrance, tears sliding down her flawless cheeks.

Duke reasoned that it would have been very easy either to turn on his heel and walk in another direction, or just to pick up speed, look straight ahead and get the hell out of there before the Kelley girl looked up.

Especially since she seemed so withdrawn and lost to the world.

He'd be doing her a favor, Duke told himself, if he just

ignored this pretty heart-wrenching display of sadness. Nobody liked looking this vulnerable. God knew that he wouldn't.

Not that he would actually cry in public—or private for that matter. When he came right down to it, Duke was fairly certain that he *couldn't* cry, period. No matter what the situation was.

Hell, he'd pretty much been the last word in stoic. But then, he thought, he'd had to be, seeing as how things hadn't exactly gone all that well in his life—or his family's life—up to this point.

Every instinct he had told Duke he should be moving fast, getting out of Susan's range of vision. Now. Yet it was as if his feet had been dipped in some kind of super-strong glue.

He couldn't make them move.

He was lingering. Why, he couldn't even begin to speculate. It wasn't as though he was one of those people who was bolstered by other people's displays of unhappiness. He'd never believed in that old adage about misery loving company. When he came right down to it, he'd never had much use for misery, his own or anybody else's. For the most part, he liked keeping a low profile and staying out of the way.

And he sure as hell had no idea what to do when confronted with a woman's tears—other than running for the hills, face averted and feigning ignorance of the occurrence. He'd never lay claim to being one of those guys who knew what to say in a regular situation, much less one where he was front-row center to a woman's tear-stained face.

But this was Susan.

Susan Kelley. He'd watched Susan grow up from an awkward little girl to an outgoing, bright-eyed and bushy-tailed little charmer who somehow managed to be completely oblivious to the fact that she was as beautiful as all get out.

Susan was the one who cheered people up. She never cried. Not that he was much of an expert on what Susan did or didn't do. He just heard things. The way a man survived was to keep his eyes and his ears open, and his mouth shut.

Ever since his twin brother Damien was hauled off to jail because everyone in town believed he had killed Mark Walsh, Duke saw little to no reason to socialize with the people in Honey Creek. And Walsh was no angel. Most people had hated him. The truth of it was, if ever someone had deserved being killed, it was Walsh. Mark Walsh was nasty, bad-tempered and he cheated on his wife every opportunity he got. And Walsh and Damien had had words, hot words, over Walsh's daughter, Lucy.

Even so, Damien hadn't killed him.

Duke frowned as, for a moment, fifteen years melted away. He remembered watching the prison bars slam, separating him from Damien. He didn't know who had killed that evil-tempered waste of human flesh, but he would have bet his life that it wasn't Damien.

Now, like a magnet, his green eyes were riveted to Susan.

Damn it, what was she crying about?

He blew out an impatient breath. A woman who was that shaken up about something shouldn't be sitting by herself like that. Someone should be with her, saying something. He didn't know what, but *something*. Something comforting.

Duke looked around, hoping to ease his conscience— and not feel guilty about his desire to get away—by seeing someone approaching the sobbing little blonde.

There was no one.

She was sitting by herself, as alone as he'd ever seen anyone on this earth. As alone as *he* felt a great deal of the time.

Damn it, he didn't want to be in this position. Didn't want to have to go over.

What was the matter with him?

He didn't owe her anything. Why couldn't he just go? Go and put this scene of vulnerability behind him? He wasn't her keeper.

Or her friend.

Susan pressed her lips together to hold back another sob. She hadn't meant to break down like this. She'd managed to hold herself together all this time, through all the visits, all the dark days. Hold herself together even when she'd silently admitted, more than once, that one conclusion was inevitable. Miranda was going to die.

Die even though she was only twenty-five years old, just like her. Twenty-five, with all of life standing right before her to run through, the way a young child would run barefoot through a field of spring daisies, with enthusiasm and joy, tickled by the very act.

Instead, six months ago Miranda had heard those most dreadful of words, *You have cancer,* and they had turned out to be a death sentence rather than a battlefield she could somehow fight her way through.

Now that she'd started, Susan couldn't seem to stop crying. Sobs wracked her body.

She and Miranda were friends—best friends. It felt as if they'd been friends forever, but it only amounted to a tiny bit more than five years. Five years that had gone by in the blink of an eye.

God knows she'd tried very, very hard to be brave for Miranda. Though it got harder and harder, she'd put on a brave face every time she'd walked into Miranda's line of vision. A line of vision that grew progressively smaller and smaller in range until finally, it had been reduced to the confines of a hospital room.

The room where Miranda had died just a few minutes ago.

That was when the dam she'd been struggling to keep intact had burst.

Walking quickly, she'd made it out of Miranda's room and somehow, she'd even made it out of the hospital. But the trip from the outer doors to the parking lot where she'd left her car, that was something she just couldn't manage dry-eyed.

So instead of crossing the length of the parking lot, sobbing and drawing unwanted attention to herself, Susan had retreated to the bench off to the side of the entrance, an afterthought for people who just wanted to collect themselves before entering the tall building or rest before they attempted the drive home.

But she wasn't collecting herself, she was falling apart. Sobbing as if her heart was breaking.

Because it was.

It wasn't fair.

It wasn't fair to die so young, wasn't fair to have to endure the kind of pain Miranda had had just before she'd surrendered, giving up the valiant struggle once and for all.

Her chest hurt as the sobs continued to escape.

Susan knew that on some level, crying like this was selfish of her. After all, it wasn't as if she was alone. She had her family—large, sprawling, friendly and noisy, they were there for her. The youngest of six, she had four sisters and a brother, all of whom she loved dearly and got along with decently now that they were all grown.

The same could be said about her parents, although there were times when her mother's overly loud laments about dying before she ever saw one viable grandchild did get under her skin a little. Nonetheless, she was one of the lucky ones. She had people in her life, people to turn to.

So why did she feel so alone, so lonely? Was grief causing her to lose touch with reality? She *knew* that if she picked up the phone and called one of them, they'd be at her side as quickly as possible.

As would Linc.

She and Lincoln Hayes had grown up together. He'd been her friend for years. Longer than Miranda had actually been. But even so, having him here, having *any* of them here right now, at this moment, just wouldn't take away this awful feeling of overwhelming sorrow and loss.

She supposed she felt this way because she was not only mourning the loss of a dear, wonderful friend, mourning the loss of Miranda's life, she was also, at bottom, mourning the loss of her own childhood. Because Death had stolen away her own innocence. Death had ushered in an overwhelming darkness that had never been there before.

Nothing was every going to be the same again.

And Susan knew without being told that for a long time to come, she was going reach for the phone, beginning calls she wouldn't complete, driven by a desire to share things with someone she couldn't share anything with any longer.

God, she was going to miss Miranda. Miss sharing secrets and laughing and talking until the wee hours of the morning.

More tears came. She felt drained and still they came.

Susan lost track of time.

She had no idea how long she'd been sitting on that bench, sobbing like that. All she knew was that she felt almost completely dehydrated. Like a sponge that had been wrung out.

She should get up and go home before everyone began to wonder what had happened to her. She had a wedding to cater tomorrow. Or maybe it was a birthday party. She couldn't remember. But there was work to do, menus to arrange.

And God knew she didn't want to worry her parents. She'd told them that she was only leaving for an hour or so. Since she worked at the family restaurant and still lived at home, or at least, in the guesthouse on the estate, her parents kept closer track of her than they might have had she been out somewhere on her own.

Her fault.

Everything was her fault, Susan thought, upbraiding herself.

If she'd insisted that Miranda go see the doctor when her friend had started feeling sick and began complaining of bouts of nausea coupled with pain, maybe Miranda would still be alive today instead of...

Susan exhaled a shaky breath.

What was the point? Going over the terrain again wouldn't change anything. It wouldn't bring Miranda back. Miranda was gone and life had suddenly taken on a more temporary, fragile bearing. There was no more "forever" on the horizon. Infinity had become finite.

Susan glanced up abruptly, feeling as if she was being watched. When she raised her eyes, she was more than slightly prepared to see Linc looking back at her. It wouldn't be that unusual for him to come looking for her if he thought she wasn't where she was supposed to be. He'd appointed himself her keeper and while she really did value his friendship, there was a part of her that was beginning to feel smothered by his continuous closeness.

But when she looked up, it wasn't Linc's eyes looking back at her. Nor were they eyes belonging to some passing stranger whose attention had been momentarily captured by the sight of a woman sobbing her heart out.

The eyes she was looking up into were green.

Intensely green, even with all that distance between them. Green eyes she couldn't fathom, Susan thought. The expression on the man's face, however, was not a mystery. It was frowning. In disapproval for her semi-public display of grief?

Or was it just in judgment of her?

Duke was wearing something a little more intense than his usual frown. Try as she might, Susan couldn't recall the brooding rancher with the aura of raw sexuality about him ever really smiling. It was actually hard even to summon a memory of the man that contained a neutral expression on his face.

It seemed to her that Duke always appeared to be annoyed. More than annoyed, a good deal of the time he looked angry. Not that she could really blame him. He was angry at his twin for having done what he'd done and bringing dishonor to the family name.

Or, at least that was what she assumed his scowl and anger were all about.

Embarrassed at being observed, Susan quickly wiped away her tears with the back of her hand. She had no tissues or handkerchief with her, although she knew she should have had the presence of mind to bring one or the other with her, given the situation she knew she might be facing.

Maybe she hadn't because she'd secretly hoped that if she didn't bring either a handkerchief or tissues, there wouldn't be anything to cry about.

For a moment, she was almost positive that Duke was going to turn and walk away, his look of what was now beginning to resemble abject disgust remaining on his face.

But then, instead of walking away, he began walking toward her.

Her stomach fluttered ever so slightly. Susan straightened her shoulders and sat up a little more rigidly. For some unknown reason, she could feel her mouth going dry.

Probably because you're completely dehydrated. How much water do you think you've got left in you?

She would have risen to her feet and started to walk away if she could have, but her legs felt oddly weak and disjointed, as if they didn't quite belong to her. Susan was actually afraid that if she tried to stand up, her knees would give way beneath her and she would collapse back onto the bench. Then Duke would *really* look contemptuously at her, and she didn't think she was up to that.

Not that it should matter to her *what* Duke Colton thought, or didn't think, of her, she silently told herself in the next breath. She just didn't want to look like a complete idiot, that was all. Her nose was probably already red and her eyes had to be exceedingly puffy by now.

Crossing to her, still not uttering a single word in acknowledgment of her present state or even so much as a greeting, Duke abruptly shoved his hand into his pocket, extracted something and held it out to her.

Susan blinked. Duke was holding out a surprisingly neatly folded white handkerchief.

When she made no move to take it from him, he all but growled, "Here, you seem to need this a lot more than I do."

Embarrassment colored her cheeks, making her complexion entirely pink at this point. "No, that's all right," she sniffed, again vainly trying to brush away what amounted to a sheet's worth of tears with the back of her hand.

"Take it." This time he did growl and it was an unmistakable command that left no room for refusal or even wavering debate.

Sniffing again, Susan took the handkerchief from him and murmured a barely audible, "Thank you."

He said nothing for a moment, only watched her as she slid the material along first one cheek and then the other, drying the tear stains from her skin.

When she stopped, he coaxed her on further, saying, "You can blow your nose with it. It won't rip. I've used it myself. Not this time," he corrected uncomfortably. "It's been washed since then."

A glimmer of a smile of amusement flittered across her lips. Susan couldn't begin to explain why, but she felt better. A lot better. As if the pain that had been growing inside of her had suddenly abated and begun shrinking back down to a manageable size.

She was about to say something to him about his kindness and about his riding to the rescue—something that seemed to suit his tall, dark, closed-mouth demeanor—when she heard someone calling out her name.

Linc. She'd know his voice anywhere. Even when it had an impatient edge to it.

The next moment, Linc was next to her, enveloping her in a hug. Without meaning to, she felt herself stiffening. She didn't want to be hugged. She didn't want to be pitied or treated like some fragile child who'd been bruised and needed protection.

If he noticed her reaction, Linc gave no indication that it registered. Instead, leaving the embrace, he slipped his arm around her shoulders, still offering protection.

"There you are, Susan. Everyone's worried about you," he said, as if he was part of her family. "I came to bring you home," he announced a bit louder than he needed to. And then his voice took on an affectionate, scolding tone. "I told you that you shouldn't have come here without me." Still holding her to him, he brushed aside a tear that she must have missed. "C'mon, honey, let's get you out of here."

A while back, she'd allowed their friendship to drift toward something more. But it had been a mistake. She didn't feel *that* way about Linc. She'd tried to let him down gently, to let him know politely that it was his friendship she valued, that there was never going to be anything else between them. But Linc seemed not to get the message. He seemed very comfortable with the notion of taking control of her life.

She found herself chafing against that notion and feeling restless.

He was being rude and completely ignoring Duke, she thought. Duke might not care, but *she* did.

Susan turned to say something to the rancher, to thank him for his handkerchief and his thoughtfulness, but when she looked where he'd just been, he was gone.

He'd left without saying another word to her.

The next moment, Linc was ushering her away, leading her toward the parking lot. She heard him talking to her, saying something about how relieved he was, or words to that effect.

But her mind was elsewhere.

Chapter 2

"You really shouldn't try to face these kinds of things alone, Susan," Linc quietly chided her as he guided Susan to his car. Once beside the shiny silver convertible, he stopped walking. "I'm here for you, you know that. And I'll *always* be here for you," he told her with firm enthusiasm.

"Yes, I know that." Fidgeting inside, Susan looked around the lot, trying to remember where she'd parked her own car. Linc meant well, but she really wanted to be by herself right now. "And I appreciate everything you're trying to do, Linc, but—"

Her voice trailed off for a moment. How did she tell him that he was crowding her without sounding as if she was being completely ungrateful? He was only trying to be kind, to second-guess her needs, she knew all that. But despite all that, despite his good intentions and her understanding, it still felt as if he was sucking up all the oxygen around her and she just couldn't put up with that right now.

Maybe later, when things settled down and fell into place she could appreciate Linc for what he was trying to do, but right now, she felt as if she desperately needed her space, needed to somehow make peace with this sorrow that kept insisting on finding her no matter which way she turned.

Linc opened the passenger door, but she continued to stand there, scanning the lot. He frowned. "What are you looking for?"

"My car." Even as she said it, Susan spotted her silver-blue four-door sedan. She breathed a sigh of relief.

He opened the passenger door wider, silently insisting that she get inside. "You're not up to driving, Susan. I'll take you home."

Her eyes met his. Susan did her best to keep her voice on an even keel, even though her temper felt suddenly very brittle.

"Don't tell me what I can or can't do, Linc. I can drive. I *want* to drive my car," she told him with emphasis.

He pantomimed pressing something down with both hands. Her temper? Was that what he was insinuating? She felt her temper flaring.

"Don't get hysterical, Susan," he warned.

The words, not to mention the action, were tantamount to waving a red flag in front of her. If the words were meant to subdue her, they achieved the exact opposite effect.

"I am *not* hysterical, Linc," she informed him firmly, "I just want to be alone for a while."

"You didn't look very alone a couple of minutes ago."

For a moment she thought he was going to pout, then abruptly his expression changed, as if he'd suddenly come up with an answer that satisfied him. "Was he bothering you?"

Susan stared at Linc, confused and wondering how he'd come to that kind of conclusion. Based on what? "Who?" she wanted to know.

"That Colton guy. You know who I mean. His brother killed Lucy Walsh's father," he said impatiently, trying to remember the man's name. "Duke," he finally recalled, then asked again as he peered at her face, "Was he bothering you?"

She felt as if Linc was suddenly interrogating her. Not only that, but she felt rather defensive for Duke, although she really hadn't a clue as to why. She'd had a crush on him when she was a teenager, but that was years in the past.

Still, he'd stopped and given her a handkerchief when he didn't have to.

"No, what makes you say that?"

Linc's shoulders rose and fell in a spasmodic shrug. "Well, you just said you wanted to be alone, and when I found you, he was in your face—"

Susan was quick to interrupt him. Linc had a tendency to get carried away. "He wasn't in my face, Linc. He hardly said a whole sentence."

Linc's expression told her that it hadn't looked that way from where he was standing. "Then he was just staring at you?"

Susan didn't like the tone that Linc was taking with her. He was invading her private space, going where he had no business venturing. He was her friend, not her father or her husband. And even then he wouldn't have the right to act this way.

"In part," she finally said. "Look, he saw I was crying and he gave me his handkerchief. No questions, nothing, just his handkerchief."

Linc snorted. "Lucky for you he didn't try strangling you with it."

It was a blatant reference to one of the theories surrounding Mark Walsh's death. The county coroner had said that it appeared Mark Walsh had been strangled, among other things, before his face was bashed in, the latter being the final blow that had ushered death in.

Susan just wanted to get away, to mourn her best friend's passing in peace, not be subjected to this cross-examination that Linc seemed determined to conduct. She lifted her chin stubbornly. "Duke's not Damien," she pointed out.

The look on Linc's face was contemptuous, both of her statement and of the man it concerned.

"I dunno about that. They say that twins have an unnatural connection. Maybe he's *just* like his brother." Linc drew himself up, squaring his shoulders before issuing a warning. "I don't want you talking to Duke Colton or having anything to do with him."

For a second, even with the emotional pain she was trying to deal with, Susan could feel her temper *really* flaring. Linc was making noises like a possessive *boyfriend*, and that was the last thing on earth she needed or wanted right now. "Linc, it's not your place to tell me what to do or not do."

Realizing the tactical error he'd just committed,

Linc tried to backtrack as quickly as he could and still save face.

"Sure it is," he insisted. "I care about you, Susan. I care about what happens to you. We don't know what these Coltons are really capable of," he warned. "And I'd never forgive myself if anything happened to you because I didn't say something."

Did Linc really think she was so clueless that she needed guidance? That she was so naive that she was incapable of taking charge of her own life? From out of nowhere a wave of resentment surged within her. She struggled to tamp it down.

She was just upset, Susan told herself. And Linc did mean well, even if he could come across as overbearing at times.

It took effort, but she managed to force a smile to her lips. "I'll be all right, Linc. Don't worry so much. And I'm still driving myself home," she added in case he thought he'd talked her out of that.

She could see that Linc didn't like her refusing his help, but he made no protest and merely nodded his head. She was about to breathe a sigh of relief when Linc unexpectedly added, "All right, I'll follow you."

Susan opened her mouth to tell him that he really didn't have to put himself out like that, but she had a feeling that she'd just be wasting her breath, and she was in no mood to argue.

Maybe she was being unfair. Another woman would have been thrilled to have someone voluntarily offer to all but wrap her in cotton and watch over her like this. There was a part of her that thought she'd be thrilled, as well. But now, coming face to face with it, she found it almost suffocating. All she wanted to do was run away.

Maybe she was overreacting, making too much of what was, at bottom, an act of kindness. But if she was overreacting, she did have a really good excuse. Someone she loved dearly had just died and blown a hole in her world, and it was going to take a while to come to terms with that.

Rather than prolong this no-win debate, Susan nodded. "All right, I'll see you at the house." With that, she turned and walked quickly over to where she'd parked her vehicle.

Duke watched the tall, slim, attractive young blonde make her way through the parking lot. More to the point, she was walking away from that annoying prissy little friend of hers.

Lincoln Hayes.

Now, there was a stalker in the making if he ever saw one, Duke judged. He wondered if Susan was aware of that, of what that Linc character was capable of.

Not his affair, Duke told himself in the next moment. The perky little girl with the swollen eyes was her own person. There was no reason for him to be hovering in the background like some wayward dark cloud on the horizon, watching over her. She might look like the naive girl next door, but he had a feeling that when push came to shove, Susan Kelley was a lot stronger, character-wise, than she appeared.

A fact, he had a feeling, that wouldn't exactly please Lincoln Hayes.

And even if she could be pushed around by the likes

of Hayes, what was that to him? Why did he feel this need to make sure she was all right? The girl had his handkerchief and he wanted it back. Eventually. There was absolutely no other reason to pay attention to her, to her comings and goings and to whether that spineless jellyfish, Hayes, actually turned out to be a stalker.

Annoyed with himself, with the fact that he wasn't leaving, Duke watched as Susan crossed to the extreme right side of the lot and got into her car, a neat little sedan that would have been all but useless on his own ranch. It wouldn't have been able to haul much, other than Susan and some of her skinny friends.

Her sedan came to life. Another minute and she was driving off the lot.

Rubbing his hands on the back of his jeans, Duke got into the cab of his beat-up dark-blue pickup and drove away.

"Have you been crying?"

Bonnie Gene Kelley fired the question, fueled by concern, the moment her daughter walked into the rear of Kelley's Cookhouse, the restaurant that she and her husband Donald ran and had turned into a nation-wide chain.

Seeing for herself that the answer to her question was yes, Bonnie Gene quickly crossed to her youngest child and immediately immersed herself in Susan's life. "Did you and that boy get into an argument?" she wanted to know.

Ever eager for one of her children to finally make her a grandmother, the way all her friends' children had, Bonnie Gene fanned every fire that potentially had an iron in it. In Susan's case, that iron had a name: Lincoln Hayes.

Lincoln wouldn't have been her first choice, or even her second one. Bonnie Gene liked her men more manly, the way her Donald was—or had been before the good life had managed to fatten him up. But Linc was here and he was crazy about Susan. Her daughter could do a lot worse than marry the boy, she supposed.

But if he made Susan cry, then all bets were off. She absolutely wouldn't stand for someone who could wound her youngest born to the extent of making her cry. Sophisticated and worldly—as worldly as anyone could be, given that they were living in a place like Honey Creek, Montana—her maternal claws would immediately emerge, razor-sharp and ready, whenever one of her children was hurt, physically or emotionally.

"No, Mother," Susan replied evenly, wishing she'd waited before walking into work, "we didn't get into an argument."

Part of her just wanted to dash up to her room and shut the door, the other part wanted to be enfolded in her mother's arms and be told that everything was still all right. That the sun still rose in the east and set in the west and everything in between was just fine.

Except that it wasn't. And she needed to grow up and face that.

"Is Miranda worse?" her father asked sympathetically, coming out of the large storage room where they kept the supplies and foodstuffs that were being used that day. He pushed the unlit cigar in his mouth over to the side with his tongue in order to sound more intelligible.

Focusing on her husband for a moment, Bonnie Gene allowed an annoyed huff to escape her lips. She marched over to him, plucked the cigar out of his mouth and made a dramatic show of dropping it into the uncovered trash basket in the corner. It was an ongoing tug of war between them. Donald Kelley seemed to possess an endless supply of cigars and Bonnie Gene apparently possessed an endless supply of patience as she removed and threw away each one she saw him put into his mouth.

Susan had long since stopped thinking that her father actually intended to smoke any of these cigars. In her opinion, he just enjoyed baiting her mother.

But today Susan didn't care about the game or whether her father actually smoked the "wretched things" as her mother called them. All of that had been rendered meaningless, at least for now. Her friend was dead and she was never going to see Miranda again. Her heart hurt.

"Miranda's gone," Susan said in small, quiet voice, answering her father's question.

"Gone?" he echoed. "Gone where?" When his wife gave him a sharp look, a light seemed to go on in his head and Donald realized what Susan had just told him. "Oh. *Gone.*" A chagrined expression washed over his face as he came over to his youngest child. "Susan, sweetie, I'm so sorry," he told her. The squat, burly man embraced her, a feat that had been a great deal easier in the days before his gut had grown to the size that it had.

Coming between them, Bonnie gently removed Susan

from Donald's grasp, turned the girl toward her and hugged her daughter closely.

For a moment, nothing was said. The other people in the kitchen, employees who had helped make the original restaurant the success that it was, went about their business, deliberately giving their employers and their daughter privacy until such time as they were invited to take part in whatever it was that was happening.

Still holding Susan to her chest and stroking her hair, the way she used to when she had been a little girl, Bonnie Gene said gently, "Susan, you knew this day was coming."

She had. Deep down, she had, but that didn't mean that she hadn't still hoped—fervently prayed—that it wouldn't. That a miracle would intervene.

"I know," Susan said, struggling again to regain control over her emotions, "it's just that it came too soon."

"It always comes too soon," Bonnie Gene told her daughter with the voice of experience. "No matter how long it takes to get here."

Bonnie Gene had no doubt that if Donald were to die before she did it wouldn't matter whether they'd been together for the past hundred years. It would still be too soon and she would still be bargaining with God to give her "just a little more time" with the man she loved.

"She's in a better place now, kiddo," Susan's father told her, giving her back a comforting, albeit awkward pat. "She's not hurting anymore."

Bonnie Gene looked at her husband, a flicker of impatience in her light-brown eyes. She tossed her head, sending her dark-brown hair over her shoulder. "Everyone always says that," she said dismissively.

"Don't make it any less true," Donald told her stubbornly, pausing to fish the cigar out of the trash. He brushed it off with his fingers, as if the cursory action would send any germs scattering.

Bonnie Gene's eyes narrowed as she looked at her husband over her daughter's shoulder. "You put that in your mouth, Donald Kelley," she hissed, "and you're a dead man."

Donald weighed his options. He knew his wife was passionate about him not smoking, and she seemed to be on a personal crusade these days against his beloved cigars. With a loud sigh, Donald allowed the cigar to fall from his fingers, landing back in the trash. There were plenty more cigars in the house—and a few of them stashed in various out-of-the-way places. Places that Bonnie Gene hadn't been able to find yet. He could wait.

The rear door opened and closed for a second time. All three Kelleys turned to see Linc walk in. He was accompanied by a blast of hot July air. It was like an oven outside. A hot, sticky, moist oven.

"I must have caught every red light from the hospital to the restaurant," Linc complained, addressing his words to the world at large.

Bonnie Gene felt her daughter stiffen the moment she heard Linc's voice. The reaction was not wasted on her. Her mother's instincts instantly kicked in.

Releasing Susan, she approached her daughter's self-appointed shadow. "Linc, I was wondering if you could do me a favor."

It was no secret that Linc was eager to score any brownie points with the senior Kelleys that he could. "Anything, Mrs. Kelley."

"The linen service forgot to send over five of our tablecloths. Be a dear and run over to Albert's Linens and get them." Taking the latest receipt and a note she'd hastily jotted down less than an hour ago, she handed both to Lincoln. "Nita at the service is already waiting for someone to come for them. Just show her these," she instructed.

Lincoln glanced at the receipt and the note, looking somewhat torn about the assignment he'd been given. It was obvious that he'd hoped that whatever it was that Susan's mother wanted done could be done on the premises and near Susan.

But then he nodded and promised, "I'll be right back." He looked at Susan, possibly hoping that she would offer to come with him, but she didn't. With a suppressed sigh and a forced smile, he turned on his heel and walked out of the kitchen through the same door he'd come in.

Susan looked at her mother. It completely amazed her how the woman who could drive her so absolutely crazy when the subject of marriage and babies came up could still somehow be so very intuitive.

She flashed her mother a relieved smile. "Thanks, Mom."

Bonnie Gene's eyes crinkled as she smiled with pleasure. "That's what I'm here for, honey. That's what I'm here for."

"Here for what?" Mystified, Donald looked first at his wife then at his daughter, trying to understand what had just happened. "And thanks for what?"

But rather than answer him, his wife and his daughter had gone off in completely opposite directions, leaving him to ponder his own questions as he scratched the thick, short white hair on his head. The action unintentionally drew his attention to the fact that his haircut, courtesy of his wife whom he insisted be the only one to cut his hair, was sadly lopsided. Again.

Though she'd been cutting his hair ever since they had gotten married all those years ago—originally out of necessity, now out of his need for a sense of tradition—Bonnie Gene had never managed to get the hang of cutting it evenly.

Donald didn't mind. He rather liked the way the uneven haircut made him look. He thought it made him appear rakish. Like the bad boy he'd never had time to be. And because he was who he was, the owner of a national chain of restaurants, no one ever attempted to tell him any differently.

Glancing over his shoulder in the direction that his wife had gone—to the front of the restaurant, undoubtedly to rub elbows with the customers—Donald quickly dipped into the trash basket and retrieved his cigar for a second time. This time, he didn't bother going through the motions of dusting it off. Instead, he just slipped it into his pants pocket.

With a satisfied smile, Donald assumed a deliberately innocent expression. Hands shoved into his pockets—his left protectively covering the cigar—he began to whistle as he walked toward the swinging double doors that led into the dining hall.

Life was good, he thought.

Chapter 3

The moment he'd realized that this time Boyd Arnold's discovery wasn't just a figment of his imagination, Wes had firmly sworn Boyd to secrecy. Knowing that Boyd had a tendency to run off at the mouth, words flowing as freely as the creek did in the winter after the first big snowstorm, he'd been forced to threaten the small-time rancher with jail time if he so much as breathed a word to *anyone*.

Boyd had appeared to be properly forewarned, his demeanor unusually solemn.

As for him, despite the fact that the words kept insisting on bubbling up in his throat and on his tongue, desperate for release, Wes hadn't even shared the news with his family. Not yet. He couldn't. He needed to be *absolutely* sure that the man with the partially destroyed face—he supposed the fish in the creek had to survive, too—actually *was* Mark Walsh.

There would be nothing more embarrassing, not to mention that it would also undermine the capabilities of the office of the sheriff, than to have to take back an announcement of this magnitude. After all, Mark Walsh had already been presumed murdered once and his supposed killer had been tried and sentenced. To say, "Oops, we were wrong once, but he's really dead now," wasn't something to be taken lightly.

His reasons for keeping this under wraps were all valid. But that didn't make keeping the secret to himself any easier for Wes. However, he had no choice. Until the county coroner completed his autopsy and managed to match Mark Walsh's dental records with the body that had been fished out of the creek, Wes fully intended to keep a tight lid on the news, no matter how difficult it got for him. Why dental records weren't used properly to identify the victim of the first crime was anybody's guess.

With any luck, he wouldn't have to hold his tongue for much longer. He desperately wanted to start the wheels turning for Damien's release. If the body in the morgue *was* Mark Walsh, then there was no way his older brother had killed the man over fifteen years ago. Not that he, or any of the family, including seven brothers and sisters, had ever believed that Damien was guilty. Some of the Colton men might have hot tempers, but none of them would ever commit murder. He'd stake not just his reputation but his life on that.

Damien was going to be a free man—once all that life-suffocating red tape was gotten through.

Damn, he thought, *finally.*

Deep down in his soul, he'd always known Damien

hadn't killed Mark. Been as sure of it as he was that the sun was going to rise in the east tomorrow morning.

He supposed that was one of the reasons he'd run for sheriff, to look into the case, to wade through the files that dealt with the murder and see if there was anything that could be used to reopen the case.

Now he didn't have to, he thought with a satisfied smile.

And he owed it all to Boyd, at least in a way. Granted, the body would have been there no matter what, but Boyd was the one who'd led him to it.

Who knew, if Boyd hadn't decided to sneak off and go duck-hunting—something that was *not* in season— maybe the fish would have eventually feasted on the rest of Walsh, doing away with the body and effectively annihilating any evidence that would have pointed toward Damien's innocence.

In that case, Damien would have stayed in prison, sinking deeper and deeper into that dark abyss where he'd taken up residence ever since the guilty verdict had been delivered fifteen years ago.

Wes made a mental note to call the county coroner's office later this afternoon to see how the autopsy was coming along—and give the man a nudge if he was dragging his heels. Max Crawford was the only coroner in these parts, but it wasn't as if the doctor was exactly drowning in bodies. Homicide was not a regular occurrence around here.

Smiling broadly, Wes poured himself his second cup of coffee of the morning. He was anxious to set his older brother's mind—if not his body—free. The sooner he told Damien about the discovery at Honey Creek, the sooner Damien would have hope and could begin walking the path that would lead him back home.

That had a nice ring to it, Wes thought, heading back to his desk. A really nice ring.

Miranda James had been an only child with no family. Her mother, Beth, had died two years ago, ironically from the same cancer that had claimed Miranda—and her father had taken off for parts unknown less than a week after Miranda was born, declaring he didn't have what it took to be a father. Because there was no one else to do it, Susan had taken upon herself all the funeral arrangements.

Bonnie Gene had offered to help, but one look at her daughter's determined face told the five foot-six, striking woman that this was something that Susan needed to do herself. Respectful of Susan's feelings, Bonnie Gene had backed away, saying only that if Susan needed her, she knew where to find her.

Susan was rather surprised at this turn of events, since her mother was such a take-charge person, but she was relieved that Bonnie Gene had backed off. It was almost cathartic to handle everything herself. Granted, it wasn't easy, juggling her full-time work schedule and the myriad of details that went into organizing the service and the actual burial at the cemetery, but she wasn't looking for easy. Susan was looking for right. She wanted to do right by her best friend.

Wanted, if Miranda *could* look down from heaven, to have her friend smile at the way the ceremony had come together to honor her all-too-brief life.

So, three days after she'd sunk down on the bench

outside the hospital, crying and trying to come to grips with the devastating loss of her best friend, Susan was standing at Miranda's graveside, listening to the soft-voiced, balding minister saying words that echoed her own feelings: that the good were taken all too quickly from this life, leaving a huge hole that proved to be very difficult to fill.

Only half listening now, Susan ached all over, both inside and out. In the last three days, she'd hardly gotten more than a few hours sleep each night, but she had not only the satisfaction of having made all the funeral arrangements but also of not dropping the ball when it came to the catering end of the family business.

As far as the latter went, her mother had been a little more insistent that she either accept help or back off altogether, but Susan had remained firm. Eventually, it had been Bonnie Gene who had backed off. When she had, there'd been a proud look in her light-brown eyes.

Having her mother proud of her meant the world to Susan. Especially right now.

Susan looked around at the mourners who filled the cemetery. It was, she thought, a nice turnout. All of Miranda's friends were here, including mutual friends, like Mary Walsh. And, not only Susan's parents, Donald and Bonnie Gene, but her four sisters and her brother had come to both the church service and the graveside ceremony.

They'd all come to pay their respects and to mourn the loss of someone so young, so vital. If she were being honest with herself, Susan was just a little surprised that so many people had actually turned up. Surprised and very pleased.

See how many people liked you, Miranda? she asked silently, looking down at the highly polished casket. *Bet you didn't know there were this many.*

Susan glanced around again as the winches and pulleys that had lowered the casket into the grave were released by the men from the funeral parlor. At the last moment, she didn't want to dwell on the sight of the casket being buried. She preferred thinking of Miranda lying quietly asleep in the casket the way she had viewed her friend the night before at the wake.

That way—

Susan's thoughts abruptly melted away as she watched the tall, lean rancher make his way toward her. Or maybe he was making his way toward the cemetery entrance in order to leave.

Unable to contain her curiosity, Susan moved directly into Duke's path just before he passed her parents and her.

"What are you doing here?" she asked.

It was a sunny day, and it was probably his imagination, but the sun seemed to be focusing on Susan's hair, making some of the strands appear almost golden. Duke cleared his throat, wishing he could clear his mind just as easily.

Duke minced no words. He'd never learned how. "Same as you. Paying my last respects to someone who apparently meant a great deal to you. I figure she had to be a really nice person for you to cry as much as you did when she died."

Susan took a deep, fortifying breath before answering him.

"She was," she replied. "A *very* nice person." She watched as the minister withdrew and the crowd began to thin out. The mourners had all been invited to her parents' house for a reception. "It just doesn't seem fair."

Duke thought of his twin brother, of Damien spending the best part of his life behind bars for a crime he *knew* beyond a shadow of a doubt his brother hadn't committed. They were connected, he and Damien. Connected in such a way that made him certain that if Damien had killed Walsh the way everyone said, he would have known. He would have *felt* it somehow.

But he hadn't.

And that meant that Damien hadn't killed anyone. Damien was innocent, and, after all this time, Duke still hadn't come up with a way to prove it. It ate at him.

"Nobody ever said life was fair," he told her in a stoic voice.

Susan didn't have the opportunity to comment on his response. Her mother had suddenly decided to swoop down on them. More specifically, on Duke.

"Duke Colton, what a lovely surprise," Bonnie Gene declared, slipping her arm through the rancher's. "So nice of you to come. Such a shame about poor Miranda." The next moment, she brightened and flashed her thousand-watt smile at him. "You are coming to the reception, aren't you?" she asked as if it was a given, not a question.

Duke had had no intentions of coming to the reception. He still wasn't sure what had prompted him to come to the funeral in the first place. Maybe it had been the expression he'd seen on Susan's face. Maybe, by being here, he'd thought to ease her burden just a little. He really didn't know.

He'd slipped into the last pew in the church, left before the mourners had begun to file out and had stood apart, watching the ceremony at the graveside. Had there been another way out of the cemetery, he would have used that and slipped out as quietly as he had come in.

Just his luck to have bumped into Susan and her family. Especially her mother, who had the gift of gab and seemed intent on sharing that gift with every living human being with ears who crossed her path.

He cleared his throat again, stalling and looking for the right words. "Well, I—"

He got no further than that.

Sensing a negative answer coming, Bonnie Gene headed it off at the pass as only she could: with verve and charm. And fast talk.

"But of course you're coming. My Donald oversaw most of the preparations." She glanced toward her husband, giving him an approving nod. "As a matter of fact, he insisted on it, didn't you, dear?" she asked, turning her smile on her husband as if that was the way to draw out a hint of confirmation from him.

"I—"

Donald Kelley only managed to get out one word less than Duke before Bonnie Gene hijacked the conversation again.

Because of the solemnity of the occasion, Bonnie Gene was wearing her shoulder-length dark-brown hair up. She still retained the deep, rich color without the aid of any enhancements that came out of a box and required rubber gloves and a timer, and she looked approximately fifteen years younger than the sixty-four years that her birth certificate testified she was—and she knew it. Retirement and quilting bees were not even remotely in her future.

Turning her face up to Duke's—separated by a distance of mere inches, she all but purred, "You see why you have to come, don't you, Duke?"

It was as clear as mud to him. "Well, ma'am—not really." Duke made the disclaimer quickly before the woman could shut him down again.

The smile on her lips was gently indulgent as she momentarily directed her attention to her husband. "Donald is his own number-one fan when it comes to his cooking. He's prepared enough food to feed three armies today," she confided, "and whatever the guests don't eat, he will." Detaching herself from Duke for a second, she patted her husband's protruding abdomen affectionately. "I don't want my man getting any bigger than he already is."

Dropping her hand before Donald had a chance to swat it away, she reattached herself to Duke. "So the more people who attend the reception, the better for my husband's health." Bonnie Gene paused, confident that she had won. It was only for form's sake—she knew men liked to feel in control—that she pressed. "You will come, won't you?"

It surprised her that the man seemed to stubbornly hold his ground. "I really—"

She sublimated a frown, keeping her beguiling

smile in place. Bonnie Gene was determined that Duke wasn't going to turn her down. She was convinced she'd seen something in the rancher's eyes in that unguarded moment when she'd caught him looking at her daughter.

Moreover, she'd seen the way Susan came to attention the moment her daughter saw Duke approaching. If that wasn't attraction, then she surely didn't know the meaning of the word.

And if there was attraction between her daughter and this stoic hunk of a man, well, that certainly was good enough for her. This could be the breakthrough she'd been hoping for. Time had a way of flying by and Susan was already twenty-five.

Bonnie Gene was nothing if not an enthusiastic supporter of her children, especially if she saw a chance to dust off her matchmaking skills.

"Oh, I know what the problem is," she declared, as if she'd suddenly been the recipient of tongues of fire and all the world's knowledge had been laid at her feet. "You're not sure of the way to our place." She turned to look at her daughter as if she had just now thought of the idea. "Susan, ride back with Duke so you can give him proper directions."

Looking over her youngest daughter's head, she saw that Linc was heading in their direction and his eyes appeared to be focused on Duke.

Fairly certain that Susan wouldn't welcome the interaction with her overbearing friend right now, Bonnie Gene reacted accordingly. Slipping her arms from around Duke's, she all but thrust Susan into the space she'd vacated.

"Off with you now," Bonnie Gene instructed, putting a hand to both of their backs and pushing them toward the exit. "Don't worry, your father and I will be right behind you," she called out.

Without thinking, Susan went on holding Duke's arm until they left the cemetery.

He made no move to uncouple himself and when she voluntarily withdrew her hold on him, he found that he rather missed the physical connection.

"I'm sorry about that," Susan apologized, falling into step beside him.

He assumed she was apologizing for her mother since there was nothing else he could think of that required an apology.

"Nothing to be sorry for," he replied. "Your mother was just being helpful."

Susan laughed. She had no idea that the straightforward rancher could be so polite. She didn't think he had it in him.

Learn something every day.

"No, she was just being Bonnie Gene. If you're not careful, Mother can railroad you into doing all sorts of things and make you believe it was your idea to begin with." There was a fondness in her voice as she described her mother's flaw. "She thinks it's her duty to take charge of everything and everyone around her. If she'd lived a hundred and fifty years ago, she would have probably made a fantastic Civil War general."

Duke inclined his head as they continued walking. "Your mother's a fine woman."

"No argument there. But my point is," Susan emphasized, "you have to act fast to get away if you don't want to get shanghaied into doing whatever it is she has planned."

"Eating something your dad's made doesn't exactly sound like a hardship to me." Donald Kelley's reputation as a chef was known throughout the state, not just the town.

Susan didn't want Duke to be disappointed. "Actually, I made a lot of it."

His eyes met hers for a brief moment. She couldn't for the life of her fathom what he was thinking. The man had to be a stunning poker player. "Doesn't sound bad, either."

The simple compliment, delivered without any fanfare, had Susan warming inside and struggling to tamp down what she felt had to be a creeping blush on the outside. Pressing her lips together, she murmured, "Well, I hope you won't be disappointed."

"Don't plan on being," he told her. Duke nodded toward the vehicle he'd left parked at the end of the lot. "Hope you don't mind riding in a truck, seeing as how you're probably used to gallivanting around in those fancy cars."

When it came down to matching dollar for dollar, the Coltons were probably richer than the Kelleys, but despite his distant ties to the present sitting president, Joseph Colton, Darius Colton didn't believe in throwing money away for show. That included buying fancy cars for his sons.

Duke was referring to Linc's sports car, Susan thought. He had to be because her own car was a rather bland sedan with more than a few miles and years on it.

But it was a reliable vehicle that got her where she had to go and that was all that ultimately mattered to her.

"I like trucks," she told him, looking at his. "They're dependable."

In response, Susan thought she saw a small smile flirt with Duke's mouth before disappearing again. And then he shrugged a bit self-consciously.

"If I'd known I'd be heading out to your place, I would've washed it first," he told her.

"Dirt's just a sign left behind by hard work," she said philosophically as she approached the passenger side of the vehicle.

Duke opened the door for her, then helped her up into the cab. She was acutely aware of his hands on her waist, giving her a small boost so that she could avoid any embarrassing mishap, given that she was wearing a black dress and high heels.

A tingle danced through her.

This wasn't the time or place to feel things like that, she chided herself. She'd just buried her best friend. This was a time for mourning, not for reacting to the touch of a man who most likely wasn't even aware that he *had* touched her.

Duke caught himself staring for a second. Staring at the neat little rear that Susan Kelley had. Funerals weren't the time and cemeteries weren't the place to entertain the kind of thoughts that were now going through his head.

But there they were anyway, taking up space, coloring the situation.

Maybe, despite the best of intentions, he shouldn't have shown up at the funeral, he silently told himself.

Too late now, Duke thought as he got into the driver's seat and started up the truck. With any luck, he wouldn't have to stay long at the reception.

Chapter 4

"Take the next turn to the—"

There was no GPS in Duke's truck because he hated the idea of being told where to turn and, essentially, how to drive by some disembodied female voice. He'd been driving around, relying on gut instincts and keen observation, for more years than were legally allowed.

For the last ten minutes he'd patiently listened to Susan issuing instructions and coming very close to mimicking a GPS.

Enough was enough. He could go the rest of the way to the Kelleys' house without having every bend in the road narrated.

"You can stop giving me directions," he told her as politely as he could manage. "I know how to get to your place."

She'd suspected as much, which was why she'd been

surprised when he'd allowed her to come along to guide him to the big house in the first place.

"If you didn't need directions, what am I doing in your truck?" she asked him.

He spared Susan a glance before looking back at the road. "Sitting."

Very funny. But at least this meant he had a sense of humor. Sort of. "Besides that."

Duke shrugged, keeping his eyes on the desolate road ahead of him. "Seemed easier than trying to argue with your mother."

She laughed. The man was obviously a fast learner as well. "You have a point."

Since she agreed with him, Duke saw no reason to comment any further. Several minutes evaporated with no exchange being made between them. The expanding silence embraced them like a tomb.

Finally, Susan couldn't take it any more. "Don't talk much, do you?"

He continued looking straight ahead. The road was desolate but there was no telling when a stray animal could come running out.

"Nope."

Obviously, he was feeling uncomfortable in her company. If her mother, ever the matchmaker, hadn't orchestrated this, he wouldn't even be here, feeling awkward like this, Susan thought. What had her mother been thinking?

"I'm sorry if you're uncomfortable," she apologized to him.

Duke spared her another glance. His brow furrowed,

echoing his confusion. "What makes you think I'm uncomfortable?"

"Because you're not talking." It certainly didn't take a rocket scientist to come to that conclusion, she thought.

Duke made a short, dismissive noise. Discomfort had nothing to do with his silence. He just believed in an economy of words and in not talking unless he had something to say. "I don't do small talk."

She was of the opinion that *everyone* did small talk, but she wasn't about to get into a dispute over it. "Okay," she acknowledged. "Then say something earth-shattering."

For a moment, he said nothing at all. Then, because she was obviously not about to let the subject drop, he asked, "You always chatter like that?"

Blowing out a breath, she gave him an honest answer. "Only when I'm uncomfortable or nervous."

"Which is it?"

Again, she couldn't be anything but honest, even though she knew that if her mother was here right now, Bonnie Gene would be rolling her eyes at the lack of feminine wiles she was displaying. But playing games, especially coy ones, had never been her thing. "Both right now."

Despite the fact that he had asked, her answer surprised him. "I make you nervous?"

He did, but oddly enough, in a good way. Rather than say yes, she gave him half an answer. "Silence makes me nervous."

He nodded toward the dash. "You can turn on the radio."

She didn't feel like hearing music right now. Somehow, after the memorial service, it just didn't seem right. What she wanted was human contact, human interaction.

"I'd rather turn you on—" As her words echoed back at her, Susan's eyes widened with horror. "I mean, if you could be turned on." Mortified, she covered her now-flushed face with her hands. "Oh, God, that didn't come out right, either."

Despite himself, the corners of his mouth curved a little. Susan looked almost adorable, flustered like that.

"That's one of the reasons I don't do small talk." He eyed her for a second before looking back at the road. "I'd stop if I were you."

"Right."

Susan took a breath, trying to regroup and not say anything that would lead to her putting her foot in her mouth again. Even so, she had to say something because the silence really was making her feel restless inside. She reverted back to safe ground: the reason he'd been at the cemetery.

"It was very nice of you to come to the funeral," she said. "Did you know Miranda well?"

He took another turn, swinging to the right. The Kelley mansion wasn't far now. "Didn't know her at all," he told her.

The answer made no sense to her. "Then why did you come?"

"I know you," he replied, as if that somehow explained everything.

She was having a hard time understanding his

reasons. "And because she was my best friend and meant so much to me, you came?" she asked uncertainly. That was the conclusion his last answer led her to, but it still didn't make any sense.

"Something like that."

But she and Duke didn't really know each other, she thought, confused. She knew *of* him, of course. Duke Colton was the twin brother of the town's only murderer. He was one of Darius Colton's boys. Each brother was handsomer than the next. And, of course, there'd been that crush she'd had on him. But she didn't really *know* him. And he didn't know her.

In a town as small as Honey Creek, Montana, spreading gossip was one of the main forms of entertainment and there were plenty of stories to spread about the Coltons, especially since, going back a number of generations, the current president of the United States and Darius Colton were both related to Teddy Colton who'd lived in the early 1900s. To his credit, the distant relationship wasn't something that the already affluent Darius capitalized on or used to up his stock. He was too busy being blustery and riding his sons to get them to give their personal best each and every day. He expected nothing less.

That kind of a demanding, thankless lifestyle might be the reason why Duke preferred keeping to himself, she reasoned.

She felt bad for him.

Following the long, winding driveway up to what could only be termed a mansion, Duke parked his pickup truck off to one side she supposed where it wouldn't be in anyone's way.

Still feeling a bit awkward, Susan announced, "We're here."

He gave her a look she couldn't begin to read. "That's why I stopped driving."

Susan waited for a smile to emerge, but his expression continued to be nondescript. She gave up trying to read his mind.

As she got out of the cab, Susan heard the sound of approaching cars directly behind them. The onslaught had begun.

"We might be first, but not by much," she observed. Within less than a minute, the driveway, large though it was, was overflowing with other vehicles, all jockeying for prime space.

The first to arrive after them were Bonnie Gene and her husband. Bonnie Gene was frowning as she looked around.

"Knew I should have hired a valet service," she reproached herself as she joined Susan and Duke. Donald came trudging up the walk several feet behind her. Since the driveway was at a slight incline, Donald was huffing and puffing from the minor exertion.

"Don't start carrying on, Bonnie Gene. People know how to park their own damn cars. No need to be throwing money away needlessly," he chided in between taking deep breaths.

Turning around to look at her husband, Bonnie Gene frowned. "Don't cuss, Donald," she chided him. "This is a funeral reception."

"I can cuss in my own house if I want to," he informed her, even though, since she'd chastised him, he knew he'd try extra hard to curb his tongue.

Bonnie Gene sighed and shook her head. "See what I have to put up with?" She addressed her question to Duke. Not waiting for a comment, she turned and raised her voice in order to be heard by the guests who had begun arriving. "C'mon everyone, let's go in, loosen our belts and our consciences just a little, and eat today as if it didn't count."

That definitely pleased Donald who laughed expansively. The deep, throaty sound could be heard above the din of voices coming from the crowd. "Now you're talking, Bonnie Gene."

His wife was quick to shoot him down. "That wasn't meant for you, Donald. That was for our guests." Keeping her "public smile" in place, Bonnie Gene uttered her threat through lips that were barely moving. "You eat any more than your allotted portion and there'll be hell to pay, Donald."

"I'm already paying it," Donald mumbled under his breath.

About to walk away, Bonnie Gene stopped abruptly and eyed her husband. "What was that?"

The look on Donald's round face was innocence personified. "Nothing, my love, not a thing."

Duke held his peace until the senior Kelleys had moved on. Once they had disappeared into the crowd filling the house, he lowered his head and asked Susan, "She always boss him around like that?"

"She does it because she loves him," Susan answered, feeling the need to be ever so slightly defensive of her mother's motives. "Mother's convinced that if she doesn't watch over him, Dad'll eat himself to death.

It's because Mother wants him around for a good long time to come that she tends to police him like that."

Duke nodded, saying nothing. Knowing that if it were him being ridden like that, he wouldn't stand for it. But to each his own. He wasn't about to tell another man how to live his life.

They'd moved inside the house by now and Duke looked around absently, noting faces. There were more people inside this room than he normally saw in a month.

He wondered how long he would have to stay before he could leave without being observed. As he was trying to come up with a time frame, his thoughts were abruptly interrupted by a flushed, flustered young woman who accidentally stumbled next to him. About to fall, she grabbed on to the first thing she could—and it was Duke.

Horrified that she'd almost pushed him over, Mary Walsh immediately apologized.

"Oh, I'm so sorry," she cried with feeling. "I didn't mean to bump into you like that." Her face was growing a deep shade of red. "New shoes," she explained, looking down at them accusingly. "I'm still a little wobbly in them."

He'd been ready to dismiss the whole thing at the word *Oh*. "No harm done," he assured her.

Drawn by the voice, Susan was quick to throw her arms around her flustered friend. "Mary, you made it after all! I wasn't sure if you were coming to the reception." She punctuated her declaration with a fierce hug.

"Yes, I made it. Just in time to step all over—" she

paused for a moment, as if searching for a name, then brightened "—Duke Colton."

The next moment Mary made the connection. A sense of awkwardness descended because she wasn't altogether sure how to react. This was Duke Colton, the brother of the man who had been convicted of killing her father. Still, manners were manners and she thoroughly believed in them.

"I really am sorry. I didn't mean to bump into you like that. New shoes," she explained to Susan in case Susan hadn't heard her a moment ago.

"She's wobbly," Duke added, looking ever so slightly amused.

"Who's wobbly?" Bonnie Gene asked, materializing amid them again with the ease of a puff of smoke. She looked from her daughter to her daughter's long-time friend, sweet little Mary Walsh.

The girl should have been married ages ago, Bonnie Gene thought. Maybe, if Mary was married, Susan wouldn't be such a stubborn holdout.

"I am, Mrs. Kelley," Mary explained. "These heels were an impulse purchase and they're too high for me. I really haven't had a chance to break them in yet," she added sheepishly.

"Well, break them in by the buffet table," Bonnie Gene urged. With a grand wave of her hand, she indicated the line that was already forming by the long table that ran along the length of the back wall. Leaning in closer to Mary, she added with enthusiasm, "Right next to that really good-looking young man in the tan jacket. See him?" she wanted to know.

"Mother," Susan cried, struggling to keep her voice low.

"Susan," Bonnie Gene responded in a sing-song voice.

She knew that none of her children appreciated her matchmaking efforts, but that was their problem, not hers. She intended to keep on trying to pair off the young people in her life wherever and whenever she had the opportunity—whether they liked it or not. People belonged in pairs, not drifting through life in single file.

Mary already knew what Susan's mother was like, but Duke undoubtedly hadn't a clue. So Susan turned toward him and said in a soft voice, "I suggest we make our getaway the minute her back is turned. Otherwise, she'll probably have you married off by midnight."

"I don't think so," Duke answered with a finality that told Susan that not only was he not in the market for a wife, he'd deliberately head in the opposite direction should his path ever cross that of a potential mate.

Susan vaguely recalled that there had been some kind of scandal last year involving Duke and an older married woman. She thought she'd heard that the woman, Charlene McWilliams, had committed suicide shortly after Duke broke things off with her.

Something of that nature would definitely have a person backing away from any sort of a relationship, even the hint of a relationship, Susan thought sympathetically.

God knew she backed away from them and she had no scandal involving a man in her past. As a matter of fact, she had nothing in her past. But there was a reason for that. She just wasn't any good at relationships.

Her forte, Susan was convinced, lay elsewhere. She was very good at her job and at raising other people's spirits. For now, she told herself, that was enough. And later would eventually take care of itself.

"There's an open bar over there." Susan pointed it out. There were a number of people, mainly men, clustering around it. She wanted to give him the opportunity to join them if that would make him feel more comfortable. "If you'd rather drink than eat, I'll understand," she added, although she doubted that would make a difference to him one way or the other.

Duke wasn't even mildly tempted. He liked keeping a clear head when he was on someone else's territory. Drinking was for winding down, for kicking back after a long, full day's work. He hadn't put in a full day yet.

"Nothing to understand," he replied. "I'd rather eat."

She couldn't exactly say why his answer had her feeling so happy, but it did.

"So would I," she agreed, flashing a wide smile at him. "Why don't I just go get us a couple of—"

She didn't get a chance to finish her sentence. Linc had swooped down on her like a hungry falcon zeroing in on his prey.

"There you are, Susan," he declared, looking relieved. "I've been looking all over for you. You shouldn't be alone at a time like this."

Oh, please, not now. Don't smother me now. She wanted to remain polite, but she wasn't sure just how long she could be that way. Linc was beginning to wear away the last of her nerves.

"I'm hardly alone, Linc," she informed him. "There're dozens and dozens of people here."

Her answer didn't deter Linc. "You know that old saying about being lonely in a crowd." He slipped his arm around her waist as comfortably as if he'd been doing it forever. At the same time, he looked smugly over at Duke. "I'll take it from here, Colton. Thanks for looking out for my girl."

She had to stop this before it went too far. Linc was being delusional. They'd dated a few times in the past, but it had gone nowhere. She thought they were both agreed on that point. Obviously not.

"I am *not* your girl, Linc," she insisted, lowering her voice so that she wouldn't embarrass him or wind up causing a scene.

She still had feelings for Linc, but they were all of the friendly variety. The romance that Linc apparently had so desperately hoped for had never materialized, although she really had tried to make herself love him the way he obviously wanted to be loved. It just wasn't meant to happen. Linc was handsome, funny and intelligent. But there was no spark, no chemistry between them. At least, she'd never been aware of any.

Apparently, Linc had been the recipient of other signals.

"You're just upset," Linc told her in the kind of soothing voice a parent used with a petulant child. "Once things get back to normal, you'll change your mind. You'll see," he promised.

"There's nothing to see," she informed him tersely,

framing her answer more for Duke's benefit than for Linc's.

But she might as well not have bothered. Linc obviously wasn't listening and Duke, when she turned to look at him, wasn't there to hear.

What is he, part bat? she silently demanded. That was twice that he'd just seemed to disappear on her. Once outside the hospital and now here. Both times, it had been just after Linc had attached himself to her side as if they were tethered by some kind of invisible umbilical chord.

Stop making excuses for him. If Duke had wanted to hang around, he would have, Susan told herself.

Besides, she had more guests to see to than just Duke Colton.

The next moment, she was saying it out loud, at least in part.

"Excuse me, Linc, but I have guests to see to," she told him, walking quickly away before he could make a comment or try to stop her obvious retreat with some inane remark.

When it came to being the perfect hostess, Susan had studied at the knee of a master—her mother. Bonnie Gene Kelley was the consummate hostess, never having been known to run out of anything, and always able to satisfy the needs and requirements of her guests, no matter what it was they wanted.

Like mother, like daughter, at least in this one respect.

Susan wove her way in and out of clusters of people exchanging memories of Miranda along with small talk. She made sure that everyone ate, that everyone drank and, just as importantly, that she didn't find herself alone with Linc again.

And all the while, she kept an eye out for Duke. She spotted him several times, always standing near someone, always seeming to be silent.

And watching her.

Their eyes met a number of times and, unlike with Linc, she felt a spark. There was definitely chemistry or *something* that seemed to come to life and shimmer between them every time she caught his eye or he caught hers.

She would have liked to put that chemistry to the test. Purely for academic purposes, of course, she added quickly.

But there was a room full of people in the way. Maybe that was the whole point, she thought suddenly. The room full of people made her feel safe. Not threatened by the tall, dark and brooding Duke.

Still…

Get a grip and focus, Susan, she upbraided herself. Her best friend was barely cold and she was exploring her options with Duke Colton. What was *wrong* with her?

She had no answer for that. Besides, right now, there was really nothing she could do about exploring any of these racing feelings any further.

And maybe that was a good thing. Everyone needed a little fantasy to spice up their lives and it only remained a fantasy if it wasn't tested and exposed to the light of day.

She was fairly certain that hers never would be. Not if Duke kept perform his disappearing act.

Chapter 5

"If I didn't know any better, I'd say you were trying to avoid me."

Startled, Susan swallowed a gasp as her heart launched into double time. She'd left the reception and come out here to the side veranda to be alone for a moment. She hadn't realized that Linc was anywhere in the immediate vicinity, much less that he'd follow her outside.

She took a deep breath to calm down. Linc was right. She *had* been avoiding him and she felt a little guilty about it. But at the same time, she felt resentful that he was making her feel that way.

Was it wrong not to want to feel hemmed in? And lately, that was the way Linc was making her feel—hemmed in. By avoiding him, she was trying to avoid having to say things she knew would hurt him.

She could see that he was hopeful that they could

"give their relationship another chance." But kissing him was like kissing her brother and that was the way she felt about him, like a sister about a brother. She cared for him, but not in *that* way.

To try to turn that feeling into something more, something sexual between them seemed more than a little icky to her. But there was no graceful way to say that, no way to avoid hurting his feelings and his ego.

So she'd been trying to avoid Linc and avoid the awkwardness that was waiting out in the wings for both of them once she made her feelings—or lack thereof—plain to him.

Susan shrugged, hoping to table the discussion until she felt more up to having it out between them. "I'm not trying to avoid you, Linc, I've just been trying to be a good hostess."

He nodded his head, as if he was willing—for now—to tolerate the excuse she was giving him. "Well, now it's time for you to think about taking care of *you*," Linc said with emphasis.

If someone had asked her about it, Susan had nothing specific to point to as to why alarms were suddenly going off in her head, but they were. Loudly.

Survival instincts had her taking a step back, away from him. She wasn't sure where he was going with this, but it had her uneasy.

"What do you mean?" she asked him.

"I mean," Linc replied patiently, like someone trying to make a mental lightweight understand his point, "that you need someone to wait on you for a change."

As he spoke, he moved in closer and didn't appear to be too happy that she was taking a step back the moment he took a step forward. Pretending not to notice, he continued moving in toward her until the three-foot-high railing that ran along the veranda prevented her from moving back any further. He'd effectively managed to corner her.

"Someone who would put your needs ahead of their own," he continued. With a smile, he slowly threaded his fingers through her hair.

Susan pulled her head back with a quick, less-than-friendly toss. He was so close to her, if she took a deep breath, her chest would be in contact with his. She didn't want to push him back, but he wasn't leaving her much of a choice.

"Linc, don't."

His voice was low, almost hypnotic as he continued talking to her. "You're confused, Susan. Your emotions are all jumbled up. You need someone to take care of you and there's nothing I'd like more than to be that someone," he told her. He bent his head so that his mouth was closer to hers.

But when he brought it down to kiss her, Susan quickly turned her head. He wound up making contact with her hair. "Linc, no."

Despite her reaction, Linc gave no sign that he was about to back off this time, or let her step aside. Instead, he coaxed, "C'mon, Susan. You know I'm the one you should be with."

She moved her head in the opposite direction, awarding him another mouthful of hair. "Linc, no," she insisted more firmly. "I want you to stop."

Her words fell on deaf ears. "Might as well give in

to the inevitable." This time, his voice was a little more forceful.

The next moment, Linc found himself stumbling backward. Someone had grabbed him by the shoulder and yanked him away as if he were nothing more than a big, clumsy rag doll.

"The lady said stop," Duke told him. His voice was deep, as if it was emerging from the bottom of a gigantic cavernous chasm. There was no missing the warning note in it.

Anger, hot and dangerous, flashed in Linc's eyes as he glared at the man who had interrupted his attempted play for Susan.

"This isn't any business of yours, Colton," he snapped at Duke.

Placing his range-toned muscular frame between Hayes and the target of Hayes' assault, Duke hooked his thumbs in his belt and directed a steely glare at the shorter man.

"Man forcing himself on a defenseless woman is everybody's business," Duke said in his steady, inflection-free voice.

Susan's chin shot up. She didn't care if this *was* Duke Colton, she was not about to be perceived as some weak-kneed damsel in distress.

"I am *not* defenseless," she protested with just enough indignation to make Duke believe that that little woman actually believed what she was saying.

She might be spunky, Duke thought, but there was no way that Susan Kelley could hold her own if Hayes decided to force himself on her. Or at least not without a weapon—or a well-aimed kick.

Still, he wasn't about to get drawn into a verbal sparring match with her over this. He'd had every intention of retrieving his truck and leaving, until he'd discovered the vehicle was barricaded in by two other cars that would have to be moved in order for him to get out. He'd been on his way to enlist Bonnie Gene's help in finding the owners of the other two vehicles when he'd seen Hayes crowding Susan.

So he shrugged now in response to Susan's protest. "Have it your way. You're not defenseless."

But Duke gave no indication that he was about to leave, at least, not until Hayes moved his butt and went back inside the house or into the hole he'd initially crawled out of.

Instead, Duke continued to stand there, his thumbs still hooked onto his belt, waiting patiently. The look in his eyes left absolutely no doubt what he was waiting for.

"I'll see you later, Susan," Linc finally bit off and then marched into the house, looking petulant and very annoyed.

Once Linc had retreated, closing the door behind him, Susan took a breath and let it out slowly. She turned toward Duke. "I suppose I should thank you."

A hint of a shrug rumbled across his broad shoulders. "You can do whatever you want to," he told her.

His seemingly indifferent words hung in the air between them as his eyes swept over her slowly. Thoroughly.

It was probably the heat and her own edgy emotional turmoil that caused her temporary foray into insanity. That was the only way she could describe it later.

Insanity.

Why else, she later wondered, would she have done what she did in response to Duke's words? Because she suddenly found herself wanting to do something that she would think in the next moment was outrageous. If she could think.

If nothing else, it was certainly out of character for her.

One minute, she was vacillating between being furious with the male species in general—both Linc and Duke acted as if they thought she was just some empty-headed nitwit who needed to be looked after.

The next minute, something inside her was viewing Duke as her knight in somewhat battered, tarnished armor. A tall, dark, brooding knight to whom she very much wanted to express her gratitude.

So she kissed him.

Without stopping to think, without really realizing what she was about to do, she did it.

On her toes, Susan grabbed onto his rock-hard biceps for leverage and support and then she pressed her lips against his.

It was a kiss steeped in gratitude. But that swiftly peeled away and before she knew it, Susan was caught up in what she'd initiated, no longer the instigator but the one who'd gotten swept up in the consequences.

That was *her* pulse that was racing, *her* breath that had vanished without backup. That was *her* head that was spinning and those were *her* knees that had suddenly gone missing in action.

Had she not had the presence of mind to anchor herself to his arms the way she had, Susan realized she might have further embarrassed herself by sinking to the ground, a mindless, palpitating mass of skin, bone and completely useless parts in between.

God, did he ever pack a wallop.

It wasn't often that Duke was caught by surprise. For the most part, he went through life with a grounded, somewhat jaded premonition of what was to come. Duke had been blessed with an innate intuition that allowed him to see what was coming at least a split second before it actually came.

It wasn't that he was a psychic; he was an observer, a student of life. And because he was a student who never forgot a single lesson he'd learned, very little out here in this small corner of the world managed to catch him by surprise.

But this had.

It had caught him so unprepared that he felt as if he'd just been slammed upside his head with a two-by-four. At least he felt that unsteady. Not only had Susan caught him completely off guard by kissing him, he was even more surprised by the magnitude of his reaction to that very kiss.

Because Charlene McWilliams' suicide over a year ago had left him reeling, he'd stepped back from having any sort of a relationship with the softer sex. Her suicide had affected him deeply, not because he'd loved her but because he felt badly that being involved with him had ultimately driven Charlene to take her own life.

Consequently, practicing mind over matter, Duke had systematically shut down those parts of himself that reacted to a woman on a purely physical level.

Or so he'd believed up until now.

Obviously he hadn't done quite as good a job shutting down as he'd thought, because this little slip of a girl— barely a card-carrying woman—had managed to arouse him to a length and breadth he hadn't been aroused to in a very long time.

Fully intending to separate his lips from hers, Duke took hold of Susan's waist. But somehow, instead of creating a wedge, he wound up pulling her to him, kissing her back.

Kissing her with feeling.

He had to create a chasm before his head spun completely out of control, Duke silently insisted, doing his best to rally.

With effort, his heart hammering like the refrain from "The Anvil Chorus," Duke forced himself to actually push Susan back—even though everything within him vehemently protested the action.

With space between them now, Duke looked at her, still stunned. And speechless.

His mind reeling and a complete blank, Duke turned on his heel and walked away from the veranda and Susan. Quickly.

The warm night breeze surrounding her like sticky gauze, Susan stood there, watching Duke grow smaller until he disappeared around the corner. Shaken, she couldn't move immediately. She wasn't completely sure if she'd just been caught up in some kind of ground-breaking hallucination or if what had just transpired— possibly the greatest kiss of all time—had been real.

What she did know was that she was having trouble breathing and that feelings both of bereavement and absolute, unmitigated joy were square-dancing inside her.

Confusing the hell out of her.

Taking as deep a breath as she could manage, Susan turned around and hurried back into the house. She needed to be able to pull herself together before she ran into her mother. One look from her mother in this present shaken-up condition and she'd be answering questions from now until Christmas.

Maybe longer.

"Where the hell have you been?" Darius Colton wanted to know.

Home to replenish his supply of water before heading back out to the range and his men again, Darius had seen his son's dusty pickup truck on the horizon, on its way to Duke's house. Like several of his other offspring, Duke lived in a house located on the Colton Ranch.

Duke had been conspicuously absent, both this morning and now part of the afternoon. He'd been absent without clearing it with him and Darius didn't like it.

Darius Colton didn't consider himself an unreasonable man, but he needed to know where everyone was and what they were doing at any given hour of the day. It was his right as patriarch of the family.

To him it was the only way to run a ranch and it was the way he'd managed to build his ranch up to what it now was.

Getting on the back of the horse he'd tethered to the rear of his truck, Darius rode up to meet Duke. Within range of the pickup, Darius pinned his son with the sharply voiced question.

When he received no answer, he barked out the question again. "I said, where the hell have you been, boy?"

Stopping the truck, Duke met his father's heated glare without flinching. He'd learned a long time ago that any display of fear would have his father pouncing like a hungry jackal on unsuspecting prey. His father had absolutely no respect for anyone who didn't stand up to him.

The confusing flip side of that was that the person who opposed him incurred his wrath. There was very little winning when it came to his father. For the most part, to get on his father's good side, a person had to display unconditional obedience and constant productivity. Anything less was not tolerated for long—if at all.

"I went to a funeral," Duke told his father, his voice even.

The answer did not please Darius. He wasn't aware of anyone of any import dying. "Well, it's going to be your own funeral you'll be attending if I catch you going anywhere again during working hours without asking me first."

"I didn't tell you because you were busy."

Duke deliberately used the word *tell* rather than *ask,* knowing that his father would pick up on the difference, but it was a matter of pride. He wanted his father to know that he wasn't just a lackey, he was a Colton and that meant he expected to be treated with respect, same as his father, even if the person on the other end of the discussion *was* his father.

His horse beside the driver's side of the truck's cab, Darius looked closely at his son. His eyes narrowed as he stared at Duke's face.

"This a frisky corpse you went to pay your respects to?" he finally asked.

There was no humor in his voice. Before Duke could ask him what he was talking about, Darius leaned in and rubbed his rough thumb over the corner of his son's lower lip.

And then he held it up for Duke's perusal.

There was a streak of pink on his father's thumb. Pink lipstick.

The same shade of lipstick he recalled Susan wearing.

"That didn't come from the corpse" was all that Duke said. And then he preemptively ran his own thumb over his lips to wipe away any further telltale signs that Susan might have left behind.

"Well, that's a relief," Darius said sarcastically. "Wouldn't want the neighbors talking." He drew himself up in the saddle. "You're way behind in your chores, boy," he informed Duke coldly. "Nobody's going to carry your weight for you."

Darius had long made it clear that he expected his offspring to work the ranch every day, putting in the long hours that were necessary. No exceptions.

"Don't expect anyone to," Duke replied. "I just came home to change," he added in case his father found fault with his coming back to his own house rather than heading directly to the range.

"Well, then, be quick about it," Darius barked. He was about to ride his horse back to his own truck parked before the big house, but he stopped for a second. Curiosity had temporarily gotten the better of him. "Whose funeral was it?"

"Miranda James," Duke answered.

Bushy eyebrows met together over a surprisingly small, well-shaped nose. Darius scowled. "Name doesn't mean anything to me."

His father's response didn't surprise him. Darius Colton didn't concern himself with anyone or anything that wasn't directly related to the range or the business of running that ranch.

"Didn't think it would," Duke said more to himself than his father.

Darius snorted, muttered something under his breath about ungrateful whelps being a waste of his time and effort, and then he rode away, leaving a cloud of dust behind in his wake.

Duke shook his head and went into the house to change. Despite the hour, he had a full day's work to catch up on. His father expected—and accepted—nothing less and he didn't want to give the man another reason to go off on him. He wasn't sure how long his own temper would last under fire.

Chapter 6

Admittedly, though it had been close to a year since he was elected sheriff, Wes was still rather new on the job. However, some things just seemed like common sense. According to the unofficial rules of procedure in cases where there was a dead body involved, the next of kin was the first to be notified.

Usually.

But in this particular troubling case, the next of kin had already *been* notified. Fifteen years ago. After getting confirmation from the county medical examiner that the body in the morgue really was Mark Walsh, Wes figured that he could put off notifying Jolene Walsh about her husband's murder for an hour or so, seeing as how this was the second time she would be receiving the news.

Since this turn of events was really disturbing—who would have thought he'd get a genuine, honest-to-God mystery so soon after being elected?—Wes wanted to turn to a sympathetic ear to run the main highlights past. Again, he didn't go the normal route. Since this case did involve his older brother, by rights the family patriarch should be the one he would go to with this.

Should be, but he didn't.

He and Darius had a prickly relationship—the same kind of relationship, when he came right down to it, that his father had with each of his children. Darius Colton, for reasons of his own that no one else was privy to, was *not* the easiest man to talk to or get along with. He never had been.

But someone in his family should be told and since this was Wes's first time notifying anyone about the death of a loved one—or, in Mark Walsh's case, a barely tolerated one—he wanted to practice it before upending Jolene Walsh's world a second time with what amounted to the same news.

So he rode out to his family's ranch and headed toward the section he knew that Duke was assigned to tending.

Wait 'til Duke hears this, Wes thought. If this didn't shake his older brother up, nothing would.

Blessed with excellent vision, Duke saw Wes approaching across the range a good distance away. Just the barest hint of curiosity reared its head as he watched his brother's Jeep grow larger.

Today was his day to mend fences—literally—and he could do with a break, Duke thought. Putting down his hammer and the new wire he was stringing across the posts, Duke left his cracked leather gloves on as he wiped the sweat from his brow with the back of his wrist.

Once he did, that brow was practically the only part of him that wasn't glistening with sweat. His shirt had long since been stripped off and was now tied haphazardly around his waist.

"Slow day in town?" he called out just before Wes pulled up beside him. "If you're tired of playing sheriff and want to do some real work, I've got another hammer around here somewhere." He glanced around to see if he'd taken the second tool out of his battered truck or left it in the flatbed.

Though no one would ever call him laid-back, Duke was considerably more at ease around his siblings, and even his nephew, his sister Maisie's son, than he was around most people. And that included his father, who he viewed as a less-than-benevolent tyrant.

When Wes made no response in return, Duke narrowed his eyes and looked at his brother more closely.

Now that he thought about it, he'd seen Wes look a lot less serious in his time.

"Who died?" he said only half in jest.

Pulling up the hand brake, Wes turned off the ignition and got out. He pulled his hat down a little lower. Out here, on the open range, the sun seemed to beat down almost mercilessly. He'd forgotten how grueling it could be out in the open like this.

"Mark Walsh," Wes answered his brother.

Duke frowned. What kind of game was this? "We already know that, Wes. Damien's in state prison doing time for it."

Wes looked up the two inches that separated him from his brother. "Damien didn't do it."

"Also not a newsflash," Duke countered. He picked up his hammer again. If Wes was out here to play games, he might as well get back to work. "Although the old man hardly lifted a finger to advance that theory." It wasn't easy, keeping a note of bitterness out of his voice. He'd always felt his father could have gotten Damien a better lawyer, brought someone in from the outside to defend his twin instead of keeping out of it the way he had. "But the rest of us know that Damien didn't do it." Bright-green eyes met blue. "Right?"

"Absolutely right," Wes said with feeling. He took a breath, then launched into his narrative. "Boyd Arnold found a body the other day in the creek."

Duke waved his hand in dismissal. He paid little attention to what went on around Honey Creek these days—even less if it involved people like Boyd Arnold.

"Did it have one head or two?" he asked sarcastically. "That lamebrain's always claiming to find these weird things—"

Wes stopped him from going on. "What he found was Mark Walsh's body."

That managed to bring Duke up short. He stared at Wes, trying to make sense out of what his brother had just told him. "Somebody dug Walsh up and then tossed him in the creek?" Nobody had ever really liked the man, but that seemed a little excessive.

Wes shook his head. "No. Whoever's in Mark Walsh's grave isn't Walsh."

Duke went from surprised to completely stunned.

He waited for a punch line. There wasn't any. "You're serious."

"Like the plague," Wes responded. "County coroner just confirmed it from Walsh's dental records. Nobody else knows yet," he cautioned, then added, "except for the coroner and Boyd, of course. Boyd's sworn to secrecy," he explained when he saw the skeptical look that came into Duke's eyes.

"That'll last ten minutes," Duke estimated with a snort. And then he realized something. "You haven't told Jolene yet?" he asked, surprised.

Wes shook his head. "Not yet. I planned to do that next. I wanted to tell you first."

Duke didn't follow his brother's reasoning. They got along all right, but he wasn't any closer to Wes than he was to some of the others. "Why me first?" Duke wanted to know.

Wes gave him an honest answer. "Because telling you is almost like telling Damien." The two weren't identical, but it was close enough. Wes sighed deeply. The guilt he bore for not being able to find something to free his brother earlier weighed heavily on his soul. "I'm going up to the county courthouse after I tell Jolene, get the wheels in motion for Damien's release."

"Why don't you go there first?" Duke suggested. He saw he'd caught Wes's attention. "Seeing how 'fast' those wheels turn, you need to get the process started as soon as possible." He gave Wes an excuse he could use to assuage his conscience. "You won't be telling Jolene anything she hasn't heard before. The only thing that's different is the timeline. She's still going to be a widow when you finish talking to her. There's no hurry to deliver the news."

Wes gave the matter a cursory thought, then nodded, won over. Duke's plan made sense. "I guess you're right."

"'Course I'm right." A small, thin smile curved Duke's lips. "I'm your big brother." And then he rolled the news over in his head as the impact of what this all meant hit. "Hell, Mark Walsh…dead again after all this time." He shook his head. "Don't that beat all? You got any idea who did it?"

Wes didn't have a clue. What he did know was the identity of the one person who didn't do it. "Not Damien."

The thin smile was replaced with a small grin on Duke's lips. "Yeah, not Damien." And that, he thought, a wave of what he assumed had to be elation washing over him, said quite a lot.

Wes checked his watch. "See you," he said, beginning to get back into his vehicle. And then, shading his eyes a little more, he stopped to squint in the direction he'd come from. "Looks like you've got company coming, Duke. This place isn't as desolate as I remember," he commented with a short laugh, getting behind the wheel of his Jeep.

Still stunned by the news Wes had delivered, even though he didn't show it, Duke looked down the road in the direction Wes had pointed.

His green eyes narrowed in slight confusion as he made out the figure behind the wheel of the silver-blue sedan.

Hell, if this kept up, they were going to need a traffic

light all the way out here, Duke thought darkly, watching Susan Kelley's little vehicle approach.

Woman didn't have enough common sense to use a truck or Jeep, he thought in disdain. Cars like hers weren't meant for this kind of road, didn't she know that?

His brother passed Susan's car, pausing a second to exchange words Duke wasn't able to make out at this distance.

He thought he saw Susan blush, but that could have just been a trick of the sunlight. The next minute, she was driving again, getting closer. This was blowing his schedule to hell.

He ran his hand through his hair, trying not to look like a wild man.

Duke wasn't wearing a shirt. She hadn't thought she'd find him like this.

Susan could feel her stomach tightening into a knot. At the same time her palms were growing damper than the weather would have warranted.

God, but he was magnificent.

For the length of a minute, Susan's mind went completely blank as her eyes swept over every inch of the glistening, rock-hard body of the man standing beside the partially completed wire fence. His worn jeans were molded to his hips, dipping down below his navel—she found her breath growing progressively shorter.

Focus, Susan, focus. The man's got other parts you could be looking at. His face, damn it, Susan, look at his face!

But that didn't exactly help, either, because Duke

Colton was as handsome as Lucifer had been reported to be—and most likely, she judged, his soul was probably in the same condition.

No, that wasn't fair, she upbraided herself. The man had come to her aid at the funeral reception. If he hadn't been there, who knew how ugly a scene might have evolved when she tried to push Linc away? She'd loudly proclaimed that she could take care of herself, but Linc outweighed her by a good fifty pounds. He could have overpowered her if he'd really wanted to.

And Duke hadn't been the one to kiss her after Linc had slunk away. She was the one who had made that fateful first move.

Duke waited until Susan was almost right there in front of him before he left the fence and walked over to her vehicle in easy, measured steps.

"Lost?" he asked her, allowing a hint of amusement to show through.

Preoccupied with thoughts that had caught her completely by surprise and made her even warmer than the weather had already rendered her, she hadn't heard him. "What?"

"Lost?" Duke repeated, then put the word into a complete sentence since her confused expression didn't abate. "Are you lost? I've never seen you this far out of town."

There was a reason for that. She'd never been this far out of town before. There hadn't been any need to venture out this way—until now.

Forcing herself to pull her thoughts together, she shook her head. "Oh. No, I'm not lost. I'm looking for you."

Suspicion was never that far away. His eyes held hers. "Why?"

She felt as if he was delving into her mind. "To apologize and to give you this."

This was a gourmet picnic basket. The general concept was something she'd been working on for a while now, attempting to sell her father on the idea of putting out a mail-order catalogue featuring some of their signature meals.

Donald Kelley was still stubbornly holding out. He thought that shipping food through the mail was ridiculous, but her mother saw merit in the idea, so currently, the "official" word was that Kelley's Cookhouse was in "negotiations" over the proposed project. The final verdict, Bonnie Gene insisted in that take charge-way of hers, was not in yet.

Duke eyed the picnic basket for a long moment before finally taking it from her. "What, exactly, are you apologizing for?" he wanted to know.

It wasn't often that she found herself apologizing for anything. The main reason for that was that she never did anything that was out of the ordinary—or exciting. Until now.

"The other afternoon," she told him, lowering her eyes and suddenly becoming fascinated with the dried grass that was beneath her boots.

"The whole afternoon, or something in particular?" Duke asked, his expression giving nothing away as he looked at her.

He was going to make this difficult for her, she thought. She should have known he would. Duke Colton had never been an easygoing man.

"For you feeling as if you had to come to my rescue," she murmured, tripping over her own tongue again. He seemed to have that effect on her, she thought. But she was determined to see this through. "For me putting you on the spot by kissing you."

Pretending to be inspecting the picnic basket, Duke drew back the crisp white-and-red checkered cloth and looked inside. The aroma of spicy barbecued short ribs instantly tantalized his taste buds. It mingled with the scent of fresh apple cinnamon pie and biscuits that were still warm. She must have brought them straight from the oven.

He glanced down at her. "Still haven't heard anything to apologize for," he told her. "I enjoyed taking that little weasel down a couple of pegs. As for you kissing me," his eyes slowly slid over her, "you *definitely* don't have anything to apologize for in that area."

Trying not to grow flustered beneath his scrutiny, Susan tried again. "I didn't mean to make you uncomfortable...."

Duke cut into her sentence. "You didn't," he told her simply.

Susan cleared her throat. This wasn't going as smoothly as she'd hoped. How was it that he made her feel more tongue-tied every time she tried to talk to him?

"Well, anyway, I just wanted to say thank you for being so nice."

That made him laugh. It was a sound she didn't recall ever hearing coming from him. She caught herself smiling in return.

"Nobody's ever accused me of being that," Duke

responded, more than slightly amused by the label, "but have it your way if it makes you happy."

Susan brushed her hands against the seat of her stone-washed jeans. She couldn't seem to shake the nervous, unsettled feeling that insisted on running rampant through her. The fact that he was still bare-chested, still wearing jeans that dipped precariously low on his hips, didn't help matters any. If anything, they caused her breath to back up in her lungs and practically solidify.

Try as she might, she couldn't seem to ignore his sun-toned muscles or his washboard abs. Her mouth felt as if it was filled with cotton as she tried to speak again. "They told me at the house that I'd find you out here. I asked," she tacked on and then felt like an idiot for stating the obvious.

Duke nodded at the information. "They'd be the ones to know."

She licked her overly dry lips and tried again. She definitely didn't want him thinking of her as a village idiot. She normally sounded a lot brighter than this. "What are you doing out here, working out in the sun like this?"

He was smiling now, enjoying this exchange. Ordinarily, he had no patience with flustered people, but there was something almost…cute about Susan hemming and hawing and searching for words. "Haven't found a way to turn down the sun while I do my work."

She didn't understand why he had to be out here in this heat, doing things that could just as easily be handled by a ranch hand. "Don't you have people to do this?"

One side of his mouth curved more than the other,

giving the resulting smile a sarcastic edge. "My father thinks his sons should learn how to put in a full day's work each day, every day. Besides," he added, "it saves him money if we do the work."

She thought that was awful. "But your father's the richest man in the county." She realized that sounded materialistic, not to mention incredibly callous. "I mean—"

Duke took no offense at her words. He was well aware that his father had amassed a fortune. The fact didn't mean anything to him one way or another. It certainly didn't make him feel as if he was entitled to a special lifestyle or to be regarded as being privileged. He believed in earning his way—and maybe he had his father to thank for that—if he were given to thanking his father.

He saw the blush creeping up her neck. "You do get flustered a lot, don't you?"

She looked embarrassed by the fact. "I'm not a people-person like my mom."

He didn't think she should run herself down like that. The way she was was just fine. "No offense to your mom, but she does come on strong at times. You, on the other hand," he continued in his off-hand manner, "come on just right."

Susan felt her pulse beginning to race.

More.

If she was being honest with herself, her pulse had started racing the instant she saw Duke's naked chest. All sorts of thoughts kept insisting on forming, thoughts she was struggling very hard not to explore.

Right now, she was just barely winning the battle. Emphasis on the word *barely*.

She licked her lips again, fearing that they might stick together in mid sentence if she didn't. "I—um—I've got to be going."

By now he'd reached into the basket and plucked out a short rib. He glanced into the interior. He could probably transfer the rest of the food into the cab of his truck, out of the sun, not that in this heat it would buy him much time.

"Want the basket back?" he offered.

"No!" she heard herself saying a bit too forcefully. *Calm down, Susan.* "I mean, that's yours. A token of my appreciation."

She'd said that already, hadn't she? Or had she? She couldn't remember. It was as if he'd just played jump rope with her brain and absolutely everything was tied up in a huge, tangled knot.

Duke nodded. "It's good," he told her, holding the short rib aloft. "But I considered any debt already paid by your first token of appreciation."

Confused, she was about to ask what token he was talking about when it hit her. He was referring to when she'd kissed him.

Pleased, embarrassed and breathless, she could only smile in response. Widely.

The next moment, she was back in the car and driving away. Quickly. She thought it was definitely safer that way. Otherwise, she ran the risk of ruining the moment by tripping over her own tongue. Again.

Chapter 7

Going to the county seat to officially file Mark Walsh's autopsy report with the court had taken longer than Wes had expected. He didn't mind. There was a certain rush that came from knowing that he could finally—finally— get Damien free, and he savored it.

He'd known all along in his gut that Damien hadn't killed that worthless SOB.

Granted, he could have saved himself a lot of time if he had called the information in over the phone or started the ball rolling via the computer, but Wes had always favored the personal touch. In this highly technical electronic age, he felt that human contact was greatly underestimated. It was easy enough to ignore an e-mail or a phone message, but not so easy to ignore a man standing outside your office door, his hat in his hand. The gun strapped to his thigh didn't exactly hurt, either.

But doing it in person had caused him to be rather late getting back to Honey Creek. He'd been gone the better part of the day and a growling stomach was now plaintively asking him to stop in town for dinner before ultimately heading toward the ranch and the small house where he lived.

The old sheriff, he knew, would have put notifying Jolene Walsh off until some time tomorrow, tending to his own needs first. After all, as Duke had said, it wasn't like telling Jolene that her husband was dead was actually going to be much of a surprise to the woman. And there certainly wasn't anything to mourn over. Everyone in town felt that Mark Walsh had been a nasty-tempered womanizer who'd had an ugly penchant for young girls. Moreover, Walsh made no secret of the fact that he'd treated Jolene more like an indentured servant than a wife throughout their marriage.

There hadn't been a single redeeming quality about the man. He hadn't even been smart, just lucky. Lucky that he had picked the right man to run his company.

His CFO, Craig Warner, was and always had been the real brains behind Walsh Enterprises. It was Warner, not Walsh, who had turned the relatively small brewery located right outside of town into a nationally known brand to be reckoned with.

But somewhere along the line, Walsh must have stumbled across a cache of brains no one else knew he had acquired. How else had he managed to fake his own death and pull it off all these years, hiding somewhere in the vicinity? Someone had finally done away with the man, but it had taken them fifteen years to do it.

But why, Wes couldn't help wondering, had the

original murder been faked to begin with? What was Walsh trying to accomplish?

And what was *he* missing?

Tired, resigned to his duty, Wes brought his vehicle to a stop before the Walsh farmhouse. Jolene had gone on living there after her husband had been murdered. The first time, Wes added silently.

It was late and he was hungry, but it just wouldn't seem right to him if he put this off until morning. She had a right to know about this latest, bizarre twist and the sooner Jolene Walsh was informed of this actual murder of her husband, the sooner she could begin to get over it. Or so he hoped.

There were several lights on in the large, rambling house. Walsh wouldn't have recognized the place if he'd had occasion to stumble into it, Wes mused. Five years after the man's supposed death, Jolene had had some major renovations done to the house, utilizing some of the profits that the business was bringing in.

Jolene had become a different woman since Walsh had vanished from her life, Wes thought. More cheerful and vibrant. She smiled a lot these days and there was a light in her eyes that hadn't been there when Walsh was around. It was good to see her that way.

This was going to knock her and Craig for a loop, Wes thought, wishing he didn't have to be the one to break this to the woman. But he couldn't very well postpone it or shirk his duty.

Standing on the front porch, Wes rang the doorbell. Then rang it again when no one answered.

He was about to try one more time before calling it a night when the door suddenly opened. Mark Walsh's widow—rightfully called that now, he couldn't help thinking—was standing in the doorway, her slender body wrapped in a cream-colored robe that went all the way down to her ankles. Her long hair was free of its confining pins and flowed over her shoulders and down her back like a red sea.

Warm amber eyes looked at him in confusion a beat before fear entered them. She was a mother and thought like one.

"Is it one of the children?" she asked. She had four, the youngest of whom, Jared, was twenty-five and hardly a child, but to Jolene, they would always be her children no matter how many decades they had tucked under their belts. And she would always worry about them.

"No, ma'am," Wes said respectfully, removing his hat. Uncomfortable, he ran the rim through his hands. "I'm afraid I've got some really strange news."

She hesitated for a moment, as if debating the invitation she was about to extend to him, then moved aside from the doorway. "Would you like to come in, Sheriff?"

He didn't plan on staying long. He had no desire to see how this news was going to affect her once the shock of it faded. "Maybe it'd be better if I didn't." He took a short breath. "Mrs. Walsh, your husband's body turned up in the creek the other day."

She stared at him as if the words he was saying were not computing.

"Turned up?" she echoed. "Turned up from where?" Horror entered her expressive eyes. "You don't mean to tell me that someone dug up his body and—"

"No, ma'am, I don't mean to say that. According to

the county coroner, Mark Walsh has only been dead for five days."

Stunned, Jolene's mouth dropped open. "But we buried Mark almost sixteen years ago. He was definitely dead." It had been a closed-casket service. Whoever had killed her husband had done it in a rage, beating him to death and rendering him almost unrecognizable, except for his clothes and the watch on his wrist. The watch that she had given him on their last anniversary. "How is this possible?"

He tried to give her a reassuring smile. "Well, we buried *somebody* sixteen years ago, but it wasn't your husband." Wes made a mental note to have that body exhumed and an identification made—if possible—to see who had been buried there. "I'm really sorry to be the one to have to tell you this," he apologized.

Jolene looked as if the air had been completely siphoned out of her lungs and she couldn't draw enough in to replace it. For a second, he was afraid she was going to pass out. Jolene clung to the doorjamb.

"You're just doing your job," she murmured, her thoughts apparently scattering like buckshot fired at random into the air. "Do you want me to come down to make a positive I.D.?" she asked in a small voice. It was obvious that she really had no desire to take on the ordeal, but would if she had to.

"No, ma'am, there's no need." He was glad he could at least spare her that. "The coroner's already made a positive identification, using your husband's dental records. I just wanted you to hear it from me before word starts spreading in town." She looked at him blankly, as if she couldn't begin to understand what he was telling her. "Boyd Arnold was the one who found the body in the creek," he explained. "And it's only a matter of time before he lets it slip to someone. Boyd's not exactly a man who can keep a secret."

Jolene nodded, seeming not altogether sure what she was nodding about. "Do you have any idea who did it?"

"That's what I aim to find out, ma'am," Wes told her politely.

Horror returned to her expressive eyes as her thought processes finally widened just a little. "Oh, my God, Sheriff, your brother, he's been in prison all this time for killing Mark. We have to—"

He anticipated her next words and appreciated the fact that Jolene could think of Damien's situation when she was still basically in shock over what he'd just told her.

"I've already started the process of getting him released from prison," Wes assured the woman. "Again, I am sorry to have to put you through this."

"It's not your fault, Sheriff." Pale, shaken, Jolene began to close the door, retreating into her home. She felt as if she was in the middle of a bad dream. One that would continue when she woke up. "Thank you for coming to let me know," she murmured.

Shutting the door, she leaned against it, feeling incredibly confused. Incredibly drained.

Jolene shut her eyes as she tried to pull herself together. When she opened them again, she wasn't alone. Craig Warner, the man who had singlehandedly helmed the brewery into becoming a household name and the sole reason she'd become the happy woman she was, was standing beside her.

"That was the sheriff. He came to tell me that Mark wasn't dead before. But he is now." Did that sound as crazy as she thought it did?

Craig nodded. "I heard," he said quietly.

Jolene blew out a breath as she dragged her hand through her long, straight hair. At fifty, she didn't have a single gray hair to her name. Astonishing, considering the trying life she'd led until Mark had been killed—or reportedly killed, she amended silently.

Her eyes met Craig's, searching for strength. "What do I do now?"

Shirtless and wearing only jeans that he'd hastily thrown on when he'd heard the doorbell, Craig padded over to her. Linking his strong, tanned fingers through hers, he gave her hand a light tug toward the staircase.

"Come back to bed," he told her.

She couldn't pull her thoughts together. Was she to have a second funeral? Did she just have the body quietly buried? There were so many questions and she just couldn't focus.

"But, Mark—" she began in protest.

"Is dead and not going anywhere," Craig told her. "He'll still be there in the morning. And he'll still be dead. You've had a shock and you need time to process it, Jo." He kissed her lightly on the temple, then looked down at her face. "Let me help you do that."

Jolene blew out another shaky breath, then smiled a small, hesitant smile reminiscent of the way she'd once been. Craig was right. He was always right.

Without another word, she let him lead her up the

stairs back to her bedroom and the bed that had become the center of her happiness.

"You think he'll stay dead this time?" Bonnie Gene asked her husband the next afternoon. The story was all over town about Mark Walsh's second, and consequently, actual murder.

Donald Kelley was in his favorite place, the state-of-the-art kitchen that he had installed at great cost in his restaurant. Feeling creative, he was experimenting with a new barbecue sauce, trying to find something that was at once familiar yet tantalizingly different to tease the palates of his patrons. Bonnie Gene had come along with him, whether to act as his inspiration or to make sure that he didn't sample too much of his own cooking wasn't clear. But he had his suspicions.

"Who?" Donald asked, distracted. Right now, the hickory flavoring was a little too overpowering, blocking the other ingredients he wanted to come through. The pot he was standing over, stirring, was as huge as his ambitions.

"Mark Walsh," she said with an air of exasperation. Didn't Donald pay attention to anything except what went into his mouth? "That man must really have enemies, to be killed twice."

"He wasn't killed the first time," Donald pointed out, proving that he *was* paying attention. "He had to fake that."

Bonnie Gene was never without an opinion. "Most likely he faked it because he knew that someone was out to get him. And apparently they finally did. Mark Walsh is really dead this time," she told her husband with finality. "Boyd Arnold's running around town volunteering details and basking in his fifteen minutes of fame for having found the body in the creek." She shivered at the mere thought of seeing the ghoulish sight of Mark Walsh's half-decomposed body submerged in the water.

"Found whose body?" Susan asked, walking into the kitchen, order forms for future parties tucked against her chest.

She set the forms down in her section of the room. It was an oversize kitchen, even by restaurant standards, which was just the way her father liked it. The size was not without its merit for her as well. It allowed her to run the catering end of the business without getting in her father's way—or anyone else's for that matter.

Bonnie Gene swung around in her daughter's direction, delighted by Susan's obvious ignorance of the latest turn of events. There weren't all that many people left to surprise with this little tidbit.

Crossing to her, Bonnie Gene placed her arm around her daughter's slender shoulders, paused dramatically and then said, "Mark Walsh."

Susan looked at her mother, confused. "What about Mark Walsh?"

"Boyd Arnold just found his body. Well, not just," Bonnie Gene corrected herself before her husband could. "Boyd found it several days ago."

That cleared up nothing. Susan stared at her mother, trying to make sense of what she was being told. She knew that in New Orleans, whenever the floods covered the various cemeteries in that city, the waters disinterred the bodies that had been laid to rest there, but there'd been no such extreme weather aberrations here.

What was her mother talking about? "But Mr. Walsh's been dead for the last fifteen years," she protested. "His body's buried in the cemetery."

There was nothing that Bonnie Gene liked more than being right. She smiled beatifically now at her daughter. "Obviously not."

Susan jumped from fact to conclusion. "Then Damien Colton is innocent."

Donald sneaked a sample of his new sauce, then covertly slipped the ladle back into the pot and continued stirring. "It would appear so," he agreed.

Susan couldn't help thinking of all the years that Damien had lost, cooling his heels in prison for a crime he hadn't committed. The years in which a man shaped his future, made his reputation, if not his fortune. All lost because a jury had wrongly convicted him.

She looked from her mother to her father. "My God, what kind of a grudge do you think Damien's going to have against the people who put him away for something he didn't do?"

The thought had crossed Bonnie Gene's mind as well. "There's something I could live without finding out," she responded.

Susan's mind went from Damien to Duke, his twin. They said that most twins had an uncanny bond, that they felt each other's pain. That was probably why he'd been so solemn all these years, she thought. How would Duke take the news of his brother's innocence?

Or did he already know?

If he did, Duke had to be filled with mixed feelings.

She knew that he'd never believed that Damien had been the one to kill Mark Walsh and he'd turned out to be right. He had to feel good about that, she reasoned.

But now Mr. Walsh really *was* dead. Who *had* killed the man after all this time? And had someone tried to frame Duke's twin brother for that first murder?

Or maybe whoever had made it look like Mr. Walsh was killed that first time had tried to frame Duke and Damien had mistakenly been accused of the crime.

But wait a minute.

Her thoughts came to an abrupt halt. Mark Walsh *hadn't* been dead at the time and he never came forward. That meant what, that Mark Walsh had been behind all this? That he had been the one who had deliberately tried to frame Damien? Or Duke?

Why?

She had to see Duke, Susan thought suddenly. This was a huge deal. The man was going to need someone to talk to, to be his friend. He'd been there for her, albeit almost silently, but he'd made his presence known. Returning the favor was the least she could do for the man.

She made up her mind. "Mother, I don't have an event to cater today."

Bonnie Gene looked at her, trying to discern where Susan was going with this. "And your point is?" she prodded, waiting.

Susan saw that one of the kitchen staff had cocked her head in her direction, listening. She moved closer to her mother, lowering her voice. "I think I'll see if Duke Colton needs a friendly ear to talk to."

Bonnie Gene nodded. "Or any other body part

that might come into play," she commented with an encouraging smile.

No, no more matchmaking, Mother. Please. "Mother, I just want to be the man's friend if he needs one," Susan protested.

"Nobody can ever have too many friends," Bonnie Gene agreed, doing her best to keep a straight face. She failed rather badly.

Susan rolled her eyes. "Mother, you're incorrigible."

"What did I say?" Bonnie Gene asked, looking at her with the most innocent expression she could muster.

Susan turned to her other parent. "Dad, back me up here."

Her father spared her a quick glance before turning his attention back to the industrial-size pot he was standing over. He chuckled under his breath, most likely happy that someone else was drawing Bonnie Gene's fire for a change.

"This is your mother you're dealing with. You're on your own, kiddo," he told her.

Bonnie Gene raised her hands, as if she was the one surrendering. "I have no idea what you two are inferring," she declared. "But I have guests to mingle with," she told them. And with that, she crossed to the swinging doors that led out into the Cookhouse's dining room. But just as she was about to walk out, she stopped and stepped back into the kitchen.

When she turned to look at Susan, there was a very pleased smile on her lips. "Looks like you won't have to drive out of town to play good Samaritan, honey."

As was the case half the time, Susan had no idea what

her mother was talking about. "What do you mean?" she asked, crossing to her.

Bonnie Gene held one of the swinging doors partially open so that Susan could get a good look into the dining area.

"Well, unless my eyes are playing tricks on me, Duke Colton just took a seat at one of the tables in the main dining room." She let the door slip back into place. "Why don't you go see what he wants?"

That was being a bit too pushy, Susan thought, suddenly feeling nervous. "I can't just go out and play waitress."

"You can if I tell you to," Bonnie Gene countered, then turned toward the lone waitress in the kitchen. The girl was about to go on duty. "Allison here is feeling sick, aren't you, Allison?"

Confusion washed over the woman's broad face. "I'm fine, Mrs. Kelley," Allison protested with feeling.

Bonnie Gene was not about to be deterred. "See how sick she is? She's delirious." Placing both hands to Susan's back, Bonnie Gene gave her a little push out through the swinging doors. "Go, take his order. And follow it to the letter," she added, raising her voice slightly as the doors swung closed again.

"You're shameless, Bonnie Gene," Donald commented with a chuckle, never looking away from the sauce, which now was making small, bubbling noises and projecting tiny arcs of hot red liquid in the air.

"As long as I get to be a grandmother, I don't care what you call me," she told him.

With that, she went to the swinging doors to open them a crack and observe Susan and Duke—and she hoped that she would have something to observe.

Chapter 8

Duke looked up just as Susan reached the two-person booth where he had parked his lean, long frame.

"Duke, I just heard."

She was breathless, although she wasn't certain exactly why. It wasn't as if she'd rushed over to his table and she hadn't been doing anything previous to this that would have stolen the air out of her lungs, but she was definitely breathless.

Subtly, Susan drew in a deep breath to sustain herself and sound more normal.

Duke continued to look at her, arching a brow, as if he was waiting for her to finish her sentence.

So she added, "About Wes finding Mark Walsh's body. I don't know whether to congratulate you or to offer my condolences."

"Why would you feel you had to do either?" Duke

asked her in that slow, rich voice of his that seemed to get under her skin so quickly.

She shifted uncomfortably. Why did he need her to explain? "Well, because this means that Damien didn't do it."

"I already knew that," he told her, his voice deadly calm.

She had no idea how to respond to that, especially since Duke was definitely in the minority when it came to that opinion. Most of the town had thought that Damien was guilty and were quick to point out that there'd been no love lost between Damien and Mark Walsh. Matters had grown worse when Walsh had discovered that Damien was in love with his daughter, Lucy.

Never in danger of being elected Father of the Year, Walsh still wanted to control the lives of all of his offspring. None of his plans included having his oldest daughter marry a Colton and he made that perfectly clear to Damien. He was the one who had broken things up between Lucy and Damien. When Walsh was discovered beaten to death in the apartment he kept expressly for romantic trysts in Bozeman shortly afterward, everyone assumed that Damien had killed Walsh.

"Why condolences?" Duke finally asked when Susan said nothing further but still remained standing there.

She took his question as an invitation to join him. Sliding into the other seat, she faced him and knotted her fingers together before responding. "Because your brother had to spend so much time in prison for a crime he hadn't committed."

Duke lifted one shoulder in a careless shrug. "Yeah, well, that's life."

Susan stared at him, stunned. How could he sit there so calmly? Did the man have ice water in his veins? Or didn't he care? She felt excited about this turn of events and she wasn't even remotely related to Damien. As a matter of fact, she hardly remembered him. She'd been barely ten years old when Damien Colton had been sent off to prison.

"Don't you have any feelings about this?" she questioned.

"Whether I have feelings or don't have feelings about a particular subject is not up for public debate or display," he informed her in the same stony voice.

Well, that certainly put her in her place, Susan thought, stung.

Angry tears rose to her eyes and she silently upbraided herself for it. Tears, to Duke, she was certain, were undoubtedly a sign of weakness. But ever since she was a little girl, tears had always popped up when she was angry, undercutting anything she might have to say in rebuttal.

The tears always spoke louder than her words.

So rather than say anything, Susan abruptly rose and walked away.

Duke opened his mouth to call out after her. He'd caught sight of the tears and felt badly about making her cry, although for the life of him he saw no reason for that kind of a reaction on her part. But then he'd long since decided that not only were women different than men, they were completely unfathomable, their brains operating in what struck him as having to be some kind of an alternate universe.

Still, he did want to apologize if he'd somehow hurt her feelings. That hadn't been his intent. However, Bertha Aldean was sitting with her husband at the table over in the corner. A natural-born gossip, the woman was staring at him with wide, curious eyes. She was obviously hungry for something further to gossip about.

There was no way he was going to give the woman or the town more to talk about.

So he went back to scanning the menu and waited for a waitress to come and take his order. Susan Kelley was just going to have to work out what was going on in her head by herself.

"He's been alive all this time?" Damien's hand tightened on the black telephone receiver he was required to use in order to hear what his brother, Duke, was saying to him.

They were seated at a long, scarred table, soundproof glass running the length of it, separating them the way it did all the prisoners from their visitors. He was surprised at the middle-of-the-week visit from Duke. Weekdays were for doing chores on the ranch according to his father's rigid work ethic.

And he was utterly stunned by the news that Duke had brought. With a minimum of words, his twin had told him about the body that Wes had discovered.

Damien had received the news with fury.

"Yeah," Duke replied to his twin's rhetorical question.

"Until the other day. Now, according to Wes, Walsh is as dead as a doornail."

Duke saw the anger in his brother's eyes and hoped that no one else noticed. He didn't want Damien doing anything to jeopardize his release.

Damien fairly choked on his anger. "That bastard could have come forward any time in the last fifteen years and gotten me released."

"Not likely, since he hated your guts," Duke reminded him in a calm, collected voice. "And more than that," Duke pointed out, "he was afraid."

Dark-brown eyebrows narrowed over darkening green eyes. "Afraid of what? Me?"

"You, maybe," Duke acknowledged. His twin was a formidable man, especially now. He'd used all his free time to work out and build up his already considerable physique. There's always the possibility that Mark framed Damien himself, but that seems like an awful lot of trouble to go to. The victim was wearing Mark's clothing and watch. "More likely, he was afraid of whoever killed that guy they found in his apartment fifteen years ago and mistook for him. He probably figured that the killer thought the same thing, that he'd killed him—Walsh," Duke clarified. "As long as people thought he was dead, Walsh thought he was safe. If that meant that you had to stay in prison, well, Walsh probably saw that as being a bonus."

"Bonus?" Damien echoed incredulously. "What do you mean bonus?"

Duke would have thought that was self-evident. "If you were in prison, you weren't making babies with his daughter."

Damien snorted. "Small chance of that. Lucy hates my guts." She'd made that perfectly clear the last time he'd seen her. But before then…before then it had been another matter. He'd thought they really had something special, something that was meant to last.

"Because she thinks you killed her father," Duke emphasized. "That's the reason she hates you. Since you didn't, there's nothing for her to hate any more."

"It's too late," Damien said quietly. *Too late.* Too much time had been lost.

Damien scrubbed his hand over his face. Joy filtered in to mix with the rage. Impotent rage because there wasn't anyone to direct that rage toward, now that Walsh was dead. Holding the jury—and his father who should have stood up for him—accountable for his being here all these years seemed pointless.

Nonetheless, he had a feeling it was going to take him a long time to work out all these anger issues he had going on inside of him.

"How much longer do I have to stay here?" he wanted to know. "And why isn't Wes here, telling me all this himself?"

"Cut the guy a little slack, Damien," Duke said. "He's been seeing everyone he can, trying to cut through the red tape and get you released. He's always been on your side, right from the start." Duke could see how restless Damien was, so he added, "There are forms to file and procedures to follow. Nothing is ever simple."

"Throwing me into jail was," Damien said bitterly.

Damien told him what they could do with the procedures and the forms. Duke laughed shortly under his breath, then advised, "You better can that kind of talk for a while, Damien. Don't give anyone an excuse to drag their feet about letting you out of here."

The veins in Damien's neck stood out as he gripped the phone more tightly. "They *owe* me."

"No argument," Duke answered, his voice low, soothing. "But you can't start to collect if you do something to get your tail thrown back into prison. You're a free man in name only right now. Hold your peace until the rest of it catches up." His eyes held Damien's, clearly issuing a warning. "Hear me?"

Damien blew out a long, frustrated breath. "I hear you." And then the barest hint of a smile crept across his lips as the reality of it all began to sink in. "I'm really getting out?"

"You're really getting out," Duke assured him, feeling a great deal of relief himself.

"How about that," Damien said more to himself than his brother. And then he looked at his twin. "What's the old man say?"

Darius Colton's expression hadn't changed an iota when Wes had told him about the new development. Instead, he'd merely nodded and then said that he could use the extra set of hands.

Damien stared at his twin. He would have thought, after all this time, that their father would have registered some kind of positive emotion. "That's it?" he pressed.

For Damien's sake, Duke wished that there had been more. But he wasn't going to lie about it. It would only come back to bite him in the end. "That's it. He never was much of a talker," Duke reminded him.

His father hadn't come to see Damien once in all the

years that he'd been confined. "Not much of a father, either," Damien bit off.

Duke shrugged. It was what it was. There wasn't anything he could do or say to change things. "Yeah, but we already knew that."

Oh, God, not again.

The thought echoed in Susan's brain the moment she saw the dead roses on the mat outside the private entrance to her catering business. She'd gotten the wilted flowers before but hadn't thought anything of it. She'd thought it was someone's idea of a bad joke.

Preoccupied with the challenging feat of keeping an ice sculpture frozen and firm in the middle of a July heat wave long enough to look good at a reception, she hadn't seen the bouquet on the ground until she'd stepped on the roses and heard them crunching under her shoes.

Startled, she'd backed up and saw what was left of them. And the envelope lying next to them. It was the type of envelope that was used for greeting cards. But if this was like the two other times, there was no greeting card inside. Instead, there was probably a note. A note written in childish block letters that made no sense to her.

Taking a deep breath, Susan stooped down and picked up the bouquet and the envelope. Steeling herself, she opened the envelope.

Sure enough, there was a folded piece of paper tucked inside it. Taking it out, she unfolded the paper. Uneven block letters spelled out another threat, similar to the one that she'd received yesterday.

DEAD FLOWERS FOR A DEAD WOMAN.

The warning might have been downright scary if it
didn't make her so mad. She held the note up to the light.
And what do you know, the Coltons' watermark.

It wasn't Linc. As aggressive as he'd become lately,
he was too smitten to pull something like this. It wasn't
his style. She knew exactly who was behind this. It was
just the kind of thing he'd do.

Duke.

But why?

Just what was he trying to pull? Was this his obscure
way of saying that he thought she was childish, as
childish as the block letters in the message? Or was he
trying to get her to back off? But back off from what?
From expressing a few feelings about the current state
of affairs regarding his brother? She was only trying to
be neighborly.

Just what the hell did Duke Colton think he was
doing?

The more Susan thought about it, the angrier she
became.

While she willingly acknowledged that she might
not be the bravest soul God had ever created, she was
definitely *not* about to be intimidated by rotting flowers
and stupid, enigmatic notes that sounded more deranged
than anything else.

It was damn well time to put a stop to this before
she found herself knee-deep in dead roses and dried-up
thorns.

Still clutching the flowers, she marched to the
kitchen's threshold.

Since this was between meals and there was no one else around, she told her father. "I'm going out, Dad."

Donald Kelley had his back to her. He was still experimenting with the new sauce he was determined to create. Currently, he was on his sixth theme and variation of the new recipe, and he barely acknowledged that he'd heard her.

"That's nice. Have fun," Donald muttered. Reaching for the long yellow tablet he'd been making all his notations on, he crossed out an ingredient near the bottom of the list.

Susan doubted that her father had actually heard what she'd said.

But her father wasn't a problem right now. Duke was. Duke Colton was insulting her with these childish notes and bouquets of dead roses. It had to be him. Who else could it be? She had every intention of putting a stop to this behavior—and give him a piece of her mind while she was at it.

The sooner the better, she thought, storming out to her car.

A head full of steam and indignation propelling her, Susan was torn as where to go first in order to locate Duke. As luck would have it, she actually found him in the first place she looked.

Wanting to cover all bases, at the last minute, rather than going to the main house on the ranch, she'd decided to stop at his house first since it was actually closer. She'd stopped her car right in front of the front door, got out and rang his doorbell. She gave him to the count of ten.

He opened the door when she got to six.

Duke's face registered a trace of surprise when he saw her. His sister, Maisie, had said that she might be stopping by and that was who he had expected to see on his doorstep, not a five-foot-ten caterer whose brown eyes were all but shooting lightning at him.

Before he could ask Susan what had brought her out to the Colton ranch for a second time in such a short period of time, she yelled "Here!" and threw what looked like a bouquet of flowers way past their prime at his feet.

Dried petals rained right and left, marking the passage before the bouquet landed.

Duke glanced down at the all but denuded bouquet and then back up at her.

"I don't remember asking for dead flowers," he said in a voice as dry as the flowers.

"Don't try to be funny!" Susan retorted angrily, her arms crossed before her.

"All right, how about confused?" he suggested. What the hell was going on? Susan was acting as crazy, as unstable as his older sister Maisie was. He toed the bouquet. More petals came loose. "Why'd you just throw those things at me?"

Duke was behaving as if he'd actually never seen the bouquet before. Maybe the man should become an actor, she thought sarcastically. "Because you left them on my doorstep."

Her answer only confused things more, not less. "I don't believe in wasting money," he told her. "But if I did decide to give you flowers, trust me, I could afford ones that weren't so damn shriveled up."

She drew herself up indignantly. He was lying to her face, wasn't her?

Or was he?

She began to vacillate ever so slightly. Her eyes on his, she asked, "You're telling me you didn't leave those flowers on my doorstep?"

"I'm telling you I didn't leave those flowers on your doorstep," he echoed.

He saw no reason to plead his case any further. If Susan had half a brain—and he was fairly confident that the youngest of the Kelleys was a very intelligent young woman—she would realize that there was no reason for him to do something so bizarre.

A little of Susan's fire abated. "What about the note?"

"What note?" he challenged.

Digging the last missive she'd received out of her purse, she held it up in front of his face. "This note."

Taking the note out of her hand, Duke held it at the proper distance so that he was able to read it. When he did, he frowned and folded it up, then handed it back to her.

"I didn't write this," he informed her flatly.

She was beginning to believe him, but she couldn't just capitulate and back away. He might be a very good liar. She knew she wasn't experienced enough when it came to men to tell the difference.

"If you didn't write this, then who did?" she challenged.

Outwardly, her bravado remained intact, but inwardly, she knew she was beginning to lose ground. Embarrassment was starting to take hold.

He paused for exactly one second, thinking. "My first guess would be Linc."

"Linc?" she echoed incredulously. "Why would he keep sending me dead flowers?" she asked, not wanting to go there. She and Linc had been friends forever. If he actually was the one sending her these horrid bouquets, that meant that he wasn't the kind of person she thought he was. And that meant that she was completely incapable of judging *anyone's* character.

"Why would I?" Duke countered, then suddenly realized what she'd just said. "This isn't the first time you've gotten dead flowers?"

She shook her head, her straight blond hair swinging back and forth, mimicking the motion. "No. I got a bouquet of rotting roses yesterday, and one the day before that. They each had notes like this one."

Once was a stupid prank. Twice was something more. Three times meant that there was a dangerous person on the other end of those notes. She could very well need protection. "Have you gone to Wes about this?" Duke wanted to know.

She was beginning to get nervous. If Duke wasn't sending the flowers as some kind of nasty prank, then who was? She refused to think it was Linc. She'd just seen him yesterday and aside from seeming a little morose, he was the same old Linc. He *couldn't* be the one sending these notes.

"No, I haven't," she said quietly.

"Maybe you should."

She looked uneasy, he thought. He hadn't meant to scare her, but on the other hand, Susan should be aware that this might be more than just some really stupid joke.

If it did turn out to be that spineless Linc character, he was going to beat the tar out of him.

The chores and his father's obsession with having all his offspring working from sunup to sundown could wait. He felt responsible for the sliver of fear he saw entering her eyes.

After reaching into the house for his hat, he closed the door. "C'mon, I'll go with you."

It was an offer she couldn't refuse.

Chapter 9

Wes had sat quietly, unconsciously rocking ever so slightly in his chair as he listened to what the young woman his brother had brought in to see him had to say.

He could feel the hairs at the back of his head rising. Wes didn't like what he was hearing.

"And this isn't the first time you've found a note like this on your doorstep?" he asked her, indicating the envelope in the center of his desk. Taking a handkerchief, he turned the envelope over, not that he expected to notice anything now that neither he nor the other two people in the room hadn't up until now.

Susan set her mouth grimly before she shook her head. "No."

"She already told you that," Duke reminded his brother impatiently. He'd taken a seat beside Susan in front of Wes's desk, but it was obvious that he would have felt more comfortable standing, as if he had better control over a situation if he was on his feet.

"Just double-checking the facts, Duke," Wes replied mildly. He wondered if there was ever going to be a point where Duke wouldn't think of him as his little brother but as a sheriff first. Probably not. Wes directed his next question to Donald and Bonnie Gene Kelly's youngest offspring. "Do you still have the other notes somewhere?"

Susan knotted her hands in her lap and shook her head. "No. I threw them away along with the flowers." She realized now that she should have hung onto them, just in case. But it had never occurred to her that the person sending this was dangerous. "I thought it was only a stupid prank."

Wes's face remained expressionless but he nodded, taking the information in. "So what changed your mind?"

"I didn't change it," Susan contradicted. "I just got fed up and mad."

Wes continued making notes in the small spiral pad he always kept on his person, replacing it only when he filled one. He wrote in pen so that the notes wouldn't fade away before he needed them.

Eventually, the pad would find its way into a file. A real file rather than a virtual one. Computers were for law-enforcement agents who had to contend with crime in the big cities and had a lot of information to deal with. In comparison to those places, Honey Creek seemed like a hick town.

A hick town with a murderer and a possible stalker, Wes reminded himself. He finished writing down what

Susan was saying and couldn't help wondering what else would crawl out from under the rocks while he was sheriff.

"Any particular reason you thought Duke was the one sending you the notes and flowers?" he wanted to know, sparing his brother a quick, sidelong glance.

Susan drew herself up, like a schoolgirl in a classroom when things like posture and radiating a positive attitude mattered. "Not now, no."

"But before?" he coaxed sympathetically.

Slim shoulders rose and fell beneath the bright pink-and-white-striped tank top. She actually did look more like a girl in high school than the successful head of the catering division of Kelley's Cookhouse.

"I thought it was Duke's way of saying I was acting like a kid," she murmured. Looking back, she realized that her reasoning didn't make any real sense. But admittedly, she wasn't thinking as clearly as she normally did, what with dealing with Miranda's death and viewing life through new, sobered eyes.

"Now that you don't think that it's Duke anymore, do you have any new thoughts about who might be sending you these threats and dried flowers?" Wes asked gently, as if he was trying to coax words out of a witness who had just been intimidated.

Susan began to shake her head because she really couldn't think of anyone this nasty, but Duke interrupted anything she might have to say. "You should check out that Lincoln character," he suggested. There was no uncertainty in his voice.

There was only one person with that first name around the area, but Wes asked anyway, wanting to make sure.

"You mean Lincoln Hayes?" When his brother nodded his response, Wes continued questioning him. "What makes you think that Lincoln Hayes is behind this?"

"It's not Linc," Susan interjected before Duke could respond.

Duke ignored her. The woman was too soft. She probably wouldn't want to think the worst of Satan. Seeing the skeptical look on Wes's face, he gave his brother what he felt was proof. "I caught him trying to force himself on her," he nodded toward Susan, "after the funeral."

Susan waved her hand at the statement, dismissing it. "Linc has this notion that we should give dating another chance. I told him it wasn't going to work. He thought it would." Duke snorted his contempt for the man. She slid forward on her chair and tapped the envelope that she'd brought in to the sheriff. "That's not Linc's handwriting."

"He write you notes in block letters often?" Duke asked her sarcastically.

Why was it that this rancher with the hard body could get to her faster than any other human being on the face of the earth? She'd never met anyone else who could scramble her emotions so quickly, making her run hot then cold within the space of a few moments.

"No, but—"

His point made, Duke looked at his brother. "I'd check it out if I were you," he repeated firmly to Wes. "See if there're any fingerprints on the envelope or the note that belong to Hayes."

Wes raised his eyes to Duke's, his patience stretched

to what he figured was his limit. "I know what to do, Duke."

"Just makin' suggestions," Duke replied.

That was, Wes knew, as close to an apology as he would ever hear from Duke. Rather than comment, he merely nodded, then turned to Susan again.

"Anything else you can think of?" he asked her. "Something Linc or someone else might have said that would make you think that they were the one sending you these threats?"

Coming up empty, Susan shook her head. "Nothing comes to mind."

"That's all right," he told her sympathetically. "Give it some time. And if something *does* come to you, give me a call," Wes instructed. He debated his next words, then said them—just in case. "It's probably harmless—a prank like you said—but for a while," he told her, offering her an encouraging smile, "I wouldn't go anywhere alone if I were you."

Instead of the expected fearfulness, Duke was surprised to see anger entering Susan Kelley's expressive eyes. She tossed her head, once again sending her short, straight blond hair swinging back and forth about her chin.

"Honey Creek is my home, Sheriff. I'm not about to let anyone make me afraid to walk around my home," she declared fiercely.

"I'm not asking you to be afraid, Ms. Kelley, I'm asking you to be sensible. Cautious," he tagged on when she continued looking at him as if she found his choice of words offensive. "There's a lot to be said for 'better safe than sorry,' " Wes told her.

"She'll be sensible," Duke chimed in, solemnly making the promise for her.

Wes nodded. "I'll hang on to this for now," he said, indicating the envelope on his desk.

"Keep it," she replied, her voice rather cool and formal. "I was just going to throw it away anyway."

"I'll get back to you on this," Wes said, then added, "we'll find out who's behind this, Susan."

"Yeah, we will," Duke added his voice to the promise as he strode out of the one-story building that had been the sheriff's office for the last fifty-some years. It was hard to say exactly to whom he was addressing his words, his brother, Susan or some invisible force he meant to vanquish.

Right now, Susan was fit to be tied and would have wanted nothing more than just to walk away from Duke Colton, but she couldn't. She'd left her car parked in front of Duke's house and he was her ride back. She had no choice but to hurry after him.

Oh, she knew she could ask someone at the Cookhouse to drive her to the Colton Ranch so she could get her car, but she really didn't want word getting back to her mother or her father about this. Neither of them knew about the notes and the flowers and she wanted to keep it that way. She didn't want them worrying.

She also didn't want her mother finding out that she'd gone to see Duke for *any* reason. The way her mind worked, her mother would be sending out invitations to her wedding by nightfall if she suspected that there was something going on between them.

Right now, Susan thought as she wordlessly plunked herself down in the passenger seat of Duke's truck, the only thing going on between them was anger. At least there was anger on her part.

She stole a look at Duke's chiseled profile as he turned the ignition on and his truck's engine coughed to life. On Duke's part, she was willing to bet, there was nothing but complete ignorance of the offense he'd just committed.

Typical male, she thought. Her anger continued to smolder and grow, like a prairie fire feeding on shoots of grass and tearing a path through the land.

Pressing her lips together, she stared straight ahead at the road and said nothing.

She'd been quiet the entire trip back to his ranch. Not that he actually minded the quiet, Duke thought, but it seemed somehow unnatural for her. The girl was nothing if not a chatterbox.

Which meant, if he remembered his basic Women 101, that there was probably something wrong. Or at least *she* thought that there was.

Nothing occurred to him.

Duke debated not staying quiet about her silence. The purpose of this trip back was to reunite her with her car. Once that happened, then she'd be on her way. And out of his hair, so to speak.

And it wasn't as if he was given to an all-consuming curiosity. Pretty much most of the time, he couldn't care less if he knew something or not. Rabid curiosity was not one of his shortcomings.

So exactly what was it about this slip of a girl that made things so different? That made *him* behave so differently?

The question ate at him.

Duke saw his house in the distance. They'd been on Colton land for a while now, all traveled in annoying silence.

A couple of more minutes and he'd be home-free, he told himself. He'd pull up his truck beside her prissy little sedan, let her get out and then she'd be gone. And he could get back to his work and anything else he felt like getting back to.

The problem was he didn't feel like getting back to work. He felt like—

Startled, Duke abruptly clamped down his thoughts. There was absolutely no point in letting his imagination go there. He had no business thinking about that. It wasn't going to happen. Moreover, he definitely didn't want it to.

Liar.

Five minutes, just five more minutes and he'd be at the house and she'd be unbuckling. And then—

Oh, hell.

Duke turned toward her. Her face was forward and her features were almost rigid. He stifled an inward sigh. So much for letting sleeping dogs lie.

"Something wrong?" he asked her in a voice that was fairly growling.

She made no answer, which told him that he'd guessed right. Something *was* wrong. He found no triumph in being right, only annoying confusion because he hadn't a clue what was sticking in her craw.

"All right, *what's* wrong?" he demanded, sparing her a second look.

He heard her sigh.

That makes two of us, honey.

Still facing forward, Susan pressed her lips together. It had been eating away at her all the way back to his ranch.

The reason she hadn't said anything was because she knew damn well that it wouldn't do any good. It would be like banging her head against a wall. Men like Duke Colton didn't learn from their mistakes. And the reason they didn't learn from their mistakes was because they didn't believe they *made* mistakes.

He'd probably say something like, she was being too sensitive, or imagining things.

Or—

But if she didn't say anything, she silently countered, she was going to explode. The man *needed* a dressing down.

She shifted in her seat and looked at him. "I don't need you to make promises for me."

Duke silently cursed himself for saying anything. He was better off with her not talking. But now that she had, he had to respond. It was going to be like picking his way across quicksand, he just knew it. "What are you talking about?"

She might have known that he wasn't aware of his transgression. Nobody probably ever challenged him. At least no woman. "You told the sheriff that I'd 'be sensible.'"

He spared her a glance. Funny how her face seemed to glow when she got excited about something. "Well, won't you be?"

Didn't he understand anything? "Whether I will or won't be isn't the point—"

Damn but women should come with some kind of a beginner's manual. Something like *A Guide to Women for the Non-Insane*.

"So what the hell is the point?"

She did have to spell this out for him, didn't she? Susan could feel her temper fraying and growing shorter and shorter.

"The point is you have no right to think you can speak for me. You don't know the first thing about me."

"I've known you all your life," he snapped indignantly.

He actually believed that, didn't he? she thought incredulously.

"No, you've been *here* all my life. In Honey Creek," she pointed out. "But you don't know anything about me, Duke."

This time the sidelong glance was more of a glare. "I know you like picking fights."

"I'm not picking a fight," she cried, exasperated. "I'm making a point." *You big, dumb jerk. Don't you even know the difference?*

Duke snorted. "Seems like the same thing from where I'm standing."

God, but there were times when she hated being right. He *was* being obtuse. "Because you're not paying attention."

"When you say something worth listening to, then, I'll pay attention," Duke told her in his cold, offhand manner.

She suddenly shut her eyes. "What color are my eyes?" she asked him.

Approaching his house, Duke looked at her. Now

what was she doing? "What the hell does that have to do with anything?"

Susan kept her eyes shut. She intended to show Duke how wrong he was in terms that even a thick-headed idiot like him could understand.

"If you 'know' me like you claim, you've got to at least know what color my eyes are. You were just looking at me a second ago. Okay, come on, tell me. What color are they?"

He was really beginning to regret this good deed he'd undertaken. "This is stupid," he told her between gritted teeth.

Susan was not about to back off. "What color?" she demanded again, then laughed. She'd proven her point. "You don't know, do you?"

She heard him huff and half expected a cuss word to follow.

Duke surprised her.

"They're brown," he finally told her. "Chocolate brown. Warm and soft when you look at a man. Warm," he repeated, "like the inside of a pan-baked brownie fresh out of the oven on Christmas morning."

Stunned, Susan slowly opened her eyes to make sure she was still sitting next to Duke Colton and that someone else hadn't slipped into the driver's side in his place.

"Lucky guess." The two words dribbled out of her mouth in slow motion. There was absolutely no conviction to them.

"Like hell it was," he retorted.

Finally home, Duke pulled up the hand brake, put the manual transmission into Park and turned off the ignition. His engine sighed audibly before shutting down. Getting out of the cab, he rounded the hood and came over to the passenger side.

He opened the door for her. Then he took her hand and, rather roughly, "helped" her out of the truck.

To be honest with himself, he wasn't exactly sure who he was angry at. Her for stirring up feelings he wanted no part of, or himself for *having* these feelings in the first place and for not being able to rein them in the way he'd trained himself to.

After that numbing fiasco with Charlene—first the affair and then her suicide—he'd sworn to himself that he wasn't going to get caught up in any kind of a relationship again. Women just weren't worth it. A few minutes of pleasure in the middle of weeks of turmoil and grief was what it usually amounted to. Hell, it just wasn't worth it.

And then she came around, this naive little girl-next-door with the heart-shaped face. Looking at her, he would never have thought that she could get under his skin, but she had.

He still didn't understand how or why. He was ten years older than she was. Ten damn years. She was only seven years old when he'd had his first woman. Seven years old. Just a baby, nothing more.

What was he doing, having feelings for someone who was so young? Yet, there it was. He had feelings for this slip of a thing. Feelings he couldn't seem to cap or harness.

Feelings that threatened to tear him apart if he gave in to them even a little.

Yeah, like he had a choice, Duke silently mocked himself.

He bracketed her arms with his strong, calloused hands. But it was his eyes that pinned her in place, his eyes that held her prisoner.

"I know everything there is to know about you," he told her angrily, biting off each word. "I don't want to, but I do."

Pulling her into his arms, he didn't give her a chance to say anything in reply, whether to challenge him or perhaps, just possibly, to admit to having feelings for him herself, the latter being a long shot in his estimation.

Susan didn't have time to say or do anything except brace herself because, in the next second, Duke's mouth came down on hers and the world, as she knew it, exploded.

It most definitely stopped turning on its axis.

Chapter 10

Duke only meant to kiss her. It was a way of venting his feelings for a moment. Maybe he even meant to scare her away by showing her the intensity of what he was feeling.

If that was his intent, it backfired. Because he wasn't scaring her away. If anything, kissing her like this had the exact opposite effect.

And worse than that, he somehow managed to lose himself completely within his own attempt at a defensive maneuver.

She tasted sweet, like the first ripe strawberries of the summer. More than that, she caused the spark within him to burst into flame, consuming him. Making his head swirl and causing his thought processes to all but disintegrate.

What was going on certainly wasn't logical.

He sure as hell hadn't meant to push this up to the next level.

But he had, and he could feel Susan's willingness to have this happen. Could feel the way she was yielding to him, silently telling him it was all right to press on. Given that, it was impossible for him to stop. Hell, it was hard for him to maintain control, not just to take her out here, with the warm sun as a witness and the hot July breeze caressing her bare skin.

The only thing that *did* stop him was that someone might ride by at the worst time and the last thing he wanted was to embarrass her. Nor did he want to share with that passerby what he felt certain in his heart was a magnificent body.

So, as he continued pressing his lips urgently against hers, drawing his very reason for existing out of the simple act, Duke scooped her up in his arms and took the three steps up to the porch.

He didn't keep the front door locked. It wasn't so much that he trusted people as that he knew he had nothing worth stealing. Someone would have to be a fool to risk coming onto the Colton Ranch solely for the purpose of breaking into his house. There was nothing to be gained by that.

Elbowing open the door, he carried Susan inside, then closed the door with his back. Only then did he allow her feet to touch the floor.

His pulse was racing and he could have sworn that there were all sorts of fireworks, crafted by anticipation, going off inside him. Who would have ever thought—?

Duke drew his head back.

* * *

He'd stopped kissing her. Was it over? Had she done something to make him back away? To suddenly change his mind?

Because she'd thought...

Determined not to come so far only to have it abruptly end, Susan rose on her toes, framed the handsome, chiseled face between her long, slender hands and kissed him.

For a moment, she felt a surge of triumph. He was kissing her back. But then that triumph faded because he drew his head back again. This time he took her hands between his, holding them still.

His eyes delved into hers. Susan struggled to catch her breath.

"You sure?" Duke asked, looking straight into her soul.

Susan didn't want to talk, didn't want to stop. She had never felt like this before and she just wanted that feeling to continue. Wanted it to flower and grow until it reached its natural conclusion. Until he made love with her.

So instead of answering him, she started to kiss Duke again. But for the second time, he took her hands in his. His eyes were deadly serious as they pinned her in place and he repeated his question.

"Are you sure?"

"Yes," she breathed, her pulse doing jumping jacks. "I'm sure."

Well, he wished he was. But he wasn't. Wasn't sure at all that this was the right thing to do. All he knew was that he really *wanted* to be with her, wanted to make love with this fresh-faced young woman and experience that incredible feeling that ultimately defied all description.

He hadn't been with a woman since he had broken things off with Charlene and she had killed herself. Hadn't thought it worth the trouble to get to that point with a woman. Duke didn't believe in paying for sex, and getting sex any other way required putting in time. Setting down groundwork.

He wasn't interested in doing that. Wasn't interested in getting tangled up with another woman.

He really had no idea how this had managed to happen so quickly. And with a woman—a girl—he'd never even thought of in this particular light.

But he was attracted to her, there was no denying that. And he wanted her. There was no denying that, either.

She made his blood rush the way he couldn't remember it rushing in a very long time.

Susan struggled to keep from losing consciousness. She'd never, *ever* felt like this before. Never experienced passion to this level before. Never experienced the desire to go the distance and find out just what there was about this ultimate bond between a man and a woman that was so seductively compelling. An eager curiosity propelled her on.

Her relationship with Linc that brief time when they'd attempted to be more than just friends was the only other time she'd even contemplated being intimate with a man—and the moment that Linc began kissing her, she'd stopped contemplating and wound up pushing him away. There'd been no bright, swirling lights, no surges of heat coupled with all but unmanageable desire.

There had only been the deep, bone-jarring sense of disappointment.

That wasn't what was going on here.

This was a whole brand-new brave world she was entering.

The excitement she felt at every turn was almost unmanageable. It fueled her eagerness. They moved from the front hall into the living room area.

When she felt Duke's strong, sure hands on her, touching her, being familiar, caressing her with a gentleness she hadn't thought he was capable of, it almost completely undid her.

She wanted to know what those hands felt like on her bare skin.

Her own hands were shaking as she began unbuttoning his shirt. She knew what she would find underneath the material and the excitement of that knowledge was making her fumble.

Damn it, he's going to figure out you're a novice before he gets to the last part. She upbraided herself, telling herself to slow down, to be calm.

She couldn't calm down.

One of the buttons got stuck and she tugged at it to no avail, feeling inept.

"Having trouble?"

Was he laughing at her? No, Duke wasn't laughing at her she realized, raising her eyes to his face. He was smiling.

Really smiling.

She couldn't remember if she'd *ever* seen Duke without at least a partial scowl on his face.

Having no experience at lying, she went with the

truth. "I'm not used to doing this," she murmured, feeling somewhat embarrassed at her ineptitude.

The smile on the rugged face deepened. "Good," she thought she heard him say.

The next moment, he helped her take off his shirt, then proceeded to do the same with hers, employing a great deal more ease than she had used.

There was no time for hesitation, no time for thought. No time to contemplate whether she was going to regret this later. The only thing Susan knew was that she didn't regret it now, and now was all that mattered.

When the rest of their clothes were shed, Duke inclined his head toward her again. Her heart was pounding as she felt his lips skim the side of her neck, then her throat. By then, she could hardly breathe. There were all sorts of wondrous, delicious things going on within her, and Susan gave up the effort of trying to catch her breath.

All she could do was fervently hope that she wasn't going to pass out.

Hungry for the taste of him, hungry to explore everything there was about this wondrous, exciting familiarity that was unfolding before her, Susan ran her hands along the hard contours of Duke's body, thrilling to his muscularity.

Thrilling even more to the evidence of his wanting her.

She knew that someone else would have pointed out that he was just having a physical reaction, that it meant nothing.

But it meant something to her.

Because this was Duke Colton and he wanted her.

Wanted her as much as she wanted him. She felt a throbbing sensation within her inner core she'd never experienced before.

As he continued kissing Susan, acquainting himself with every inch of her, Duke found himself both wanting to go slow, to savor every second of this—and to go quickly so that he could experience the ultimate pleasure that tempted him so relentlessly.

Somehow, he managed to continue going slow.

To his surprise, he enjoyed watching her react to him, enjoyed the decidedly innocent way surprise registered on her freshly scrubbed face when he teased a climax from her using his fingertips and then his lips. Enjoyed, too, the urgency with which Susan twisted and bucked against him, seeking to absorb the sensation he'd created for her as she also gasped for air.

The expression of wonder on her face made him think that she hadn't ever—

Duke abruptly stopped what he was doing and looked at her.

Susan felt the change in him immediately. A shadow of fear fell over her and something inside her literally froze.

Her eyes flew open. "What? Why did you stop?" she cried, then immediately questioned, "Did I do something wrong?"

Troubled, Duke sat up and dragged a hand through his hair. It didn't seem possible in this day and age, and yet...

"Susan, are you a virgin?" he asked her quietly.

Susan pressed her lips together. "No," she cried with feeling.

Too much feeling, Duke thought, looking at her face. "Susan," he asked in the same tone he'd just used to inquire after her virginity, "are you lying?"

She closed her eyes for a moment and sighed. She really wasn't any good at this, she thought. Lying came so naturally to other people, why did it have to stick in her throat?

"Yes."

She couldn't read his expression. Was he angry at her? Disgusted?

"Why?" he asked.

For a moment she stared down at the cracked leather sofa they'd tumbled onto. When she raised her eyes again, there was a look of defiance in them. She had as much right to this, to making a choice, as anyone.

"Because I want it to be you," she told him. "I want you to be the first."

He needed to understand her reasoning. He wanted her to make him understand. "Why?"

Why did they have to discuss this now? Why couldn't it just happen? She was fairly certain that other women didn't have to explain themselves before they made love for the first time.

"Because I never felt this way before," she told him truthfully. "Never wanted to make love with anyone before. I promise I won't hold you to anything, won't expect anything. Not even for you to do it again," she added, her voice soft. She touched his arm, silently supplicating. "Just don't turn away from me now. Please."

He looked at her. Never in a million years would he have thought that he'd be trying to talk a woman out of making love with him. But he couldn't just take her innocence from her without trying to make her understand what she was doing.

"Susan, you don't know what you're asking. I'm not any good for you," he insisted.

Susan raised her eyes to his. "That's not for you to decide," she told him simply. "That's my decision—and I've made it."

He should have been able to get up and walk away, Duke thought. The act of lovemaking—of having sex—had never been so all consuming to him that he couldn't think straight, couldn't easily separate himself from his actions. Couldn't just cut it off with no lingering repercussions.

But this time it was different.

This time, there was something about it, about Susan, about the sweetness that she was offering up to him, that robbed him of his free will, of his ability to stop, get up and walk away. He *always* could before.

He couldn't now.

He lightly cupped her cheek with his hand, the tender expression all but foreign to him. "You're going to be sorry," he predicted.

Susan's voice was firm, confident, as she replied, "No, I'm not."

He had nothing left in his arsenal to use in order to push her away. He didn't want to push her away. Every fiber of his being suddenly wanted her, wanted the life-sustaining energy he saw contained within her. Wanted, he knew, to completely wrap himself up in her and lose himself, lose the huge weight he felt pressing down on him.

Making love with Susan made him feel lighter than air and he didn't want to surrender that. Not yet. Not until he had a chance to follow that feeling to its ultimate conclusion.

Taking her into his arms again, Duke lay back down with her. He kissed Susan over and over again until he felt as if he were having an out-of-body experience.

And when he finally couldn't hold back any longer and he entered her, the small gasp of surprise that escaped her lips almost had him pulling back. The last thing he wanted was to cause her pain.

But she wouldn't let him stop. And for a single moment, she was the strong one, not Duke. She took the choice out of his hands.

They became one, rushing to the final, all-fulfilling moment, one of body, one of soul. And when it happened, when the final burst overtook him, Duke realized that he had never felt this complete before.

He had no idea what that meant. But now wasn't the time to explore it.

He held her to him, waiting for his heart to stop pounding so hard.

Maisie Colton didn't realize she was crying until she blinked and a tear slid down her face.

She'd seen them.

Had seen them kissing.

Had seen that two-bit floozy, Susan Kelley, sinking her claws into her little brother. Into Duke. Casting a spell over him.

Five years older and six inches shorter than Duke, Maisie bore a striking resemblance to her brother, except for her dramatic aqua eyes, and she felt closer to Duke than she did to anyone.

She wasn't going to stand for it. Wasn't going to allow that Kelley slut to make off with the only person on the ranch who was her ally. Duke didn't look down his nose at her, didn't judge her the way her father and the others did. Duke understood what it felt like to be a loner. Moreover, he'd never questioned her about her son, Jeremy, never even asked her who the boy's father was. Unlike their own father, Darius, who even now never missed an opportunity to badger her about her "shameless" betrayal of the family honor.

Like her father knew anything about honor, she thought contemptuously.

It was Duke who knew about honor. Like a strong, silent knight in shining armor, Duke had always been there for her. She could actually *talk* to him, tell him how she felt about things and he'd listen to her. Listen without judging.

She'd come to rely on him a great deal.

But if Duke got mixed up with that little whore, then everything would change. She'd lose him, lose the only friend she had around here.

She'd be all alone.

Suddenly feeling cold, Maisie ran her hands up and down her arms.

It wasn't going to happen, she promised herself. Duke wasn't going to take up with that little twerp. Not if she had anything to say about it.

Not even if she had to do something drastic to Susan Kelley to make her back off.

Permanently.

They'd gone inside.

Holding her breath, Maisie made her way slowly toward the house. She had to see what they were up to, had to see if it was as bad as she thought.

Maisie hated the Kelleys, hated the idea of any of her family getting mixed up with them. She couldn't stand the idea of Susan Kelley even *talking* to her brother. If the little bitch was doing anything else, that would be so much worse.

Maisie looked around. The terrain was as flat as the pancakes she'd made for Jeremy for breakfast this morning. If anyone was coming, she'd see them. But there was no one around. No one to see what she was about to do and chastise her for it.

She had a right to protect herself, Maisie silently argued. A right to protect what was hers.

Tiptoeing over to the window beside the front door, Maisie moved in what amounted to slow motion the last foot. And then she peered into the window by degrees to ensure that they didn't see her.

Maybe there was nothing going on.

Maybe he didn't like the way she kissed.

Maisie looked in, hoping.

Praying.

Her heart froze within her chest.

Pressing her lips together to stifle a gasp, she pulled back against the wall, her heart hammering in her shallow chest.

Damn it, it was worse than she thought.

That whore was naked. Stark-naked. So was Duke. How *could* he? He was letting that little whore throw herself at him. Tempt him. Didn't he know that the little bitch was no good for him? Why wasn't he throwing her out? Telling her to leave?

She squeezed her eyes shut as more tears filled them. A sob clawed its way up her throat but she deliberately kept her mouth shut. She couldn't take a chance on them hearing her.

God but she wished she'd thought to bring her gun with her. Just to fire over that bitch's head. Just to scare her a little.

Or maybe a lot.

Susan Kelley had no right to take Duke away from her. No damn right! If her brother abandoned her, if he chose that whore over her, who was she going to talk to?

She had to find a way to scare this little two-bit whore off. And if she couldn't scare Susan off, then she was just going to have to kill her. There'd be no other choice.

The thought made Maisie smile.

Chapter 11

Dragging air into his lungs, Duke sat up on the sofa, watching Susan. Trying to reconcile what he knew about her with what he'd just discovered about her. That she seemed to have the capacity to do the impossible. She had rocked his world.

"You can stay, you know. If you want to," Duke was quick to qualify. That way, the ball was in her court and not his. He wasn't asking her to stay, he was telling her she could if she wanted to. That put the emphasis on her desire, not his.

He was having trouble wrestling with these newfound sensations and emotions and didn't want to make things worse by exposing them to public scrutiny.

Susan was gathering up her clothes from the floor as quickly as she could. Now that the passion and the ensuing euphoria had both faded away, she felt awkward.

Naked was not exactly her normal state of being. Naked made her uncomfortable.

Very uncomfortable.

Not to mention she had this strange feeling she couldn't seem to shake that they had been observed. She could have sworn that when she'd thrown back her head at one point, she'd seen something move by the window. And if there was someone outside, wouldn't they have knocked by now?

A tree branch, it was probably just a tree branch, swaying in the hot breeze, she silently insisted to herself. She was just being jumpy.

Be that as it may, Susan knew she'd feel better once she had her clothes back on. And as for Duke, well, he didn't sound as if he cared one way or another if she stayed or if she left.

So she was determined to leave while there was still a shred of dignity available to her—or for her to pretend that it was available.

"I've got to get back to the restaurant," Susan murmured in response to Duke's cavalier invitation of sorts.

"You do what you have to do," he told her matter-of-factly.

Totally unselfconscious about being stark-naked he fetched his jeans and slid them on.

Even battling embarrassment, Susan had trouble drawing her eyes away from Duke from the moment that he got up.

She couldn't help thinking that Duke Colton was one hell of a specimen of manhood.

Wearing only his jeans, barely zipped and still

unsnapped, consequently dipping precariously low on hips that put the word *sculptured* to shame, Duke turned to her. Very slowly, as if he was drawing out scattered leaves, he ran his fingers through her hair.

His eyes held hers.

She hadn't a clue as to what he was thinking or feeling.

"Sure you have to go?" he asked her.

A very firm yes! hovered on her lips, but somehow couldn't manage to emerge. The lone word was seared into place by the heat of the lightning bolts that insisted on going off inside her all over again. She could hardly even breathe.

One by one, Duke removed the clothes she was clutching against her, never looking at either them or at the bit of her that was uncovered once the clothing was cast aside. Instead, his eyes remained on hers, doing a fantastic job of unraveling her.

She finally found her tongue. It was thick and clumsy—and definitely not cooperating. "I...really... have to...go."

"If you say so," Duke murmured. Tilting her head up toward his, he brought his mouth down to hers again.

And succeeded in keeping her there for yet another go-round, another hour filled with salvos of ecstasy and brand-new peaks that begged to be explored and then went off like rocket flares.

"You know he's only toying with you."

Two days later, lost in her own world, her mind only partially on working out the menu for the next dinner she and her staff were scheduled to cater, Susan looked up, startled by the intrusion of the harsh voice.

She was in her office and although she distinctly remembered leaving her door open, it was closed now. And there was a woman in the office with her. Glaring at her.

It took Susan a moment to realize who the woman was. Maisie Colton, the oldest of eight full- and half-sibling Colton offspring. The woman looked a little wild-eyed. And not a hundred-percent mentally stable.

Susan knew all about the whispers, the rumors. Maisie Colton had borne a love child, fathered by a man she refused to name. Speculation, even now, fourteen years later, ran high and rampant as to who that man might be. But Maisie's lips were sealed.

Guarding her secret so zealously despite her father's unrelenting attempts to uncover the man's identity might be the reason that Maisie seemed to be so off-kilter these days. To everyone who dealt with her, she seemed to be two cards shy of a full deck, if not more. That was the way Susan had heard her father describe Maisie. There'd been pity in his voice when he'd said it.

There were times, like now, when Maisie appeared to be going off the deep end.

"I'm afraid I don't know what you're talking about, Maisie," Susan answered, her tone politely dismissing the woman.

But Maisie wasn't about to be brushed aside that easily. She drew herself up, looming over Susan, "Sure you do," she insisted, then fairly shouted at her. "I'm talking about my brother."

Susan raised her chin. She was *not* about to let herself be chastised.

"You have lots of brothers." Whereas she had only one and she really wished Jake was here right now to rid her of this menace.

The next moment, Susan silently upbraided herself. She was twenty-five years old, running a successful business and had, due to that romantic interlude with Duke, crossed over into the world of womanhood. It was time she stopped looking to others to champion her and took up weapons to fight her own battles.

"Duke, I'm talking about Duke!" Maisie shouted at her impatiently. "He's just toying with you. You don't mean anything to him, so why don't you save yourself a lot of grief and just stop hanging around him?" Maisie fairly spat out.

For a moment, Susan stared at the older woman. Was she guessing, or had Duke actually told her about their afternoon? Had he thought so little of her that he'd broadcast what they had done together for anyone to hear? How many other people knew?

And then, for no apparent reason, it came to her out of the blue. She had her answer. She hadn't imagined that there was someone watching them that day at Duke's house, there *had* been someone watching. Maisie.

She thought she was going to be sick.

But in the next moment, the feeling passed. Instead, Susan became angry. Very, very angry. "You watched us, didn't you?" she demanded, her eyes narrowing into blazing slits.

Taken by surprise by the accusation, Maisie had no ready answer at her disposal.

She stumbled over her own tongue, then tossed her long brown hair over her painfully thin shoulder. "What if I did?" she retorted haughtily.

Susan would have preferred to be friends with the older woman. She liked to think of herself as friendly and outgoing. The kind of woman another woman would have welcomed as a friend.

But by attacking her, Maisie left her no choice. This was *not* her fault.

"There are names for people like you," she informed Duke's unstable sister, making no secret of the disgust she was experiencing.

Nothing Susan could have actually said could have been worse than the names that were running now through Maisie's head. Names her father had flung at her more than once. Wanting to strike out, she doubled up her fists. But rather than hit Susan, Maisie uttered an angry cry and swiped her hand along Susan's desk, sending a vase of daisies crashing to the floor. The vase broke, leaving the flowers homeless.

"You'll be sorry," Maisie predicted furiously, yanking open the office door. "Wait and see, you'll be sorry."

And with that, Duke's sister slammed the door and stormed out.

Susan closed her eyes for a moment, gathering herself together. Part of her wanted to run after Maisie, to pin the thin, fragile woman down and send for the sheriff to file a complaint.

Not a wise move, she pointed out to herself. After all, the sheriff was one of Maisie's brothers.

The other part just felt sorry for Maisie. She knew that the woman had had a hard time of it, being harassed not only by the holier-than-thou people in town, but by her own father. Darius Colton allowed his daughter to live on the Colton ranch—along with her son he had never accepted into the family—but he made her pay for the so-called kindness. Made her pay for any tiny crumb he sent Maisie's way.

It made her eternally grateful for her own set of parents—even if her mother did tend to drive her insane with broad hints about not getting any younger and needing to get started on creating a family *now*, if not yesterday.

Well, if nothing else, the Coltons were certainly not a dull lot, Susan thought. Carefully getting down on her knees, she gingerly began to gather up the shards of glass that had once been a cut-glass vase.

That was the way Duke found her, on her knees, piling up pieces of glass onto a tissue that was spread out on the floor beside her desk. Opening the door in response to her wary "Come in," he took one look at the mess and crouched down to help her.

"What happened?" It was actually meant as a rhetorical question. The answer he received didn't fall into that category.

She took a breath before giving Duke an answer. "Your big sister had a 'run in' with my vase." She grimaced. "The vase lost."

Duke sat back on his heels, looking at her. "My sister?" he repeated, confused. "Maisie?"

"You have any other sisters I don't know about?" Susan asked drolly.

There was his half-sister Joan, a product of one of his father's affairs, but that's clearly not who Susan meant.

Duke frowned. Deeply. This wasn't making any sense. Why would Maisie cause a scene like this? He hadn't even thought that his sister *knew* Susan. "No, but—what was she doing here?"

Susan sighed, reliving the event in her mind. She couldn't quite separate herself from it. It had really bothered her.

"Telling me that you were just toying with me and that I should walk away if I knew what was good for me." She stopped picking up pieces of glass and looked at Duke. He wasn't reacting. "Is she right? Did you send her to warn me off?"

She couldn't fathom his expression as he looked at her. "Is that what you think?"

Susan looked up toward the ceiling, thinking. And not getting anywhere. "I don't know what to think— except that Maisie could be dangerous if she got angry enough."

If he were being honest, Duke would have to admit that there was part of him that agreed with Susan. There were times when he worried that Maisie might do something that couldn't be swept under the rug or just shrugged off. Something that would go badly and backfire on her.

But family loyalty made him feel compelled to dismiss Susan's concerns, so out loud he said, "Maisie's harmless. She's just a little off at times, that's all. But she's been through a lot and the old man hasn't exactly made life easy for her. He rides everyone, especially Maisie and she's a little fragile."

There was merit to his argument, Susan thought. But he was missing a very significant point. He might even be blind to it, she judged. "I think Maisie's afraid I might try to take you away from her."

"That's ridiculous," he scoffed. The shattered vase forgotten, Duke rose to his feet, not a little indignant over what he assumed that Susan was implying. "Why would Maisie think that? She's my sister, not some woman I've been seeing."

Susan quickly stood up and placed her hand on his chest, in part to calm him, in part to keep him from leaving before she explained herself. She hadn't meant to insult him.

"I'm not saying that's how you see her, but I think in Maisie's world, things are a little...confused. She probably looks to you as someone she can trust, someone she can share her thoughts with."

The man might be stoic, but there was a gentleness in his manner when he mentioned his sister's plight with their father. Her guess was that Duke didn't want to see Maisie hurt. She liked him for that, even if Maisie had overtly threatened her.

His eyes were angry as he promised, "I'll have a talk with her."

"Don't yell at her, Duke," Susan cautioned, in case what she'd just told him caused his temper to flare. "I think your sister is really scared." She paused for a moment, debating, then decided that Duke had a right to know what she suspected had happened. "I also think she saw us."

Duke's gaze grew very dark as he stared at her. "Saw us?" he echoed.

Now what was Susan talking about? Women were way too complicated, never coming right out and saying what was on their minds. They had to hint, to skirt around the words until a guy's head got painfully dizzy.

"Yes, *saw us*," Susan emphasized meaningfully, her eyes on his.

Because his mind didn't work that way, for a moment he didn't know what Susan meant by that cryptic phrase. And then it hit him.

"Oh."

Anger over having his privacy invaded battled with the general compassion he normally felt for his sister. He'd always cut her a lot of slack, especially after Damien had been sent to prison.

"Hell," he sighed, shaking his head, "now I really *am* going to have a talk with her." One hand on the doorknob, he was about to leave when Susan called his name.

"Duke?"

He stopped abruptly, his mind already back at the main house. "What?"

"What are you doing here?" Susan wanted to know. When he looked at her blankly, she became a little more specific. "You don't usually come into town," she pointed out. Was this a casual visit, or was there something more behind it? She knew which way she would have wanted it. She tried not to sound too eager as she asked, "Why did you come by my office?"

"I was in town on an errand." It seemed rather foolish now to say that he'd just wanted to see her. To see if he'd just imagined the whole thing back at the ranch the other day or if the sight of her actually could make his stomach feel as if it was at the center of a Boy Scout knot-tying jamboree. "Thought I'd stop by," he mumbled.

Damn, but this wasn't him, Duke thought in disgust at his own behavior. He was never tongue-tied. He was quiet by choice, not out of necessity to keep from sounding like some kind of babbling idiot. And yet, this bit of a thing had him tripping over his own tongue, badly messing with his thought processes.

What *was* it about her that made him act like a village idiot?

Pushing all thoughts of Maisie aside, Susan smiled at him as she drew closer.

"I'm glad you did," she told him. "Are you hungry?" she asked him, suddenly thinking of it. Glancing over her shoulder at the small refrigerator where she kept all sorts of samples for her catering business, Susan made him an offer. "If you are, I could just whip up something for you to nibble on, take the edge off."

What he found himself wanting to nibble on required no special preparation by Susan. All she had to do was stand there.

Where the hell had that come from?

The next moment, stifling an annoyed sigh, Duke mentally shook his head. It was official. He had become certifiably crazy. And all it had taken was two consecutive rolls in the proverbial hay with the Kelley girl.

Maybe this dropping by wasn't such a good idea. He didn't like discovering that he had these needs knocking around inside him. At least, not to this extent. He'd known he was attracted to her, but he'd figured he could keep it under control.

Time to go. "No thanks," he muttered, begging off. "I'm good."

Yes, you are, Susan thought, then realized that she could probably go straight to hell for what she was thinking right now.

Clearing her throat, she nodded in response to what he'd just said to her. "Well, thanks for stopping by. It was nice seeing you again."

"Yeah, well…" For the second time, he began leaving the office, his hand on the doorknob, ready to pull it shut behind him and make good his escape. He was almost home free when the words seemed to escape of their own volition. "You free tonight?"

Her mother had taught her that it was never a good thing to appear to be too available because that made it seem as if no one else wanted her. But no one else did, other than Linc and there was no way she wanted even to entertain that thought. Besides, her mother was a big one for playing games. Playing games had never held any appeal to her. And to that end, she just wasn't any good at it. Lies had a way of tripping her up.

"I'm free," she told him. "Why?" She crossed her fingers behind her back, hoping that the reason he was asking was because he wanted to see her.

Duke knew he was voluntarily putting a noose around his neck, but he assured himself that he could remove it at any time and would, once he grew tired of Susan. But for now, he was very far from being tired of her. "I was thinking maybe I could come by, pick you up and we could go out to eat."

He liked the way a smile came to her eyes when he asked her out. It was almost as if he could feel the warmth. "Sounds good to me."

He did his best to appear as if he was indifferent to

the actual outcome. It was rather adolescent of him, but this was a brand-new place he found himself traveling through. "So if I come by, you'll be there?"

"That better be 'when,' not 'if,'" she informed him, doing her best to sound serious and not letting him hear the way her heart was pounding, "and yes I'll be there when you come by. Oh, by the way, I'm staying in the guest house behind the main house."

Duke nodded. He understood how that was. There were amenities that were hard to give up, but they weren't worth trading hard-won independence for, either. A compromise was the best way to go. "All the comforts of home without having them underfoot."

She didn't really consider her parents being "underfoot" but it was too early in this budding whatever-it-was to admit that to him outright. He might look down at her for that.

"Something like that," she answered vaguely.

He nodded, not pressing the issue. "Seven o'clock sound all right to you?"

"Seven o'clock sounds fine." Hesitating, Susan knew she'd have no peace about the evening ahead unless she asked. "Maisie won't be coming with you, will she?"

"Don't worry," he assured her. "She'll be staying home tonight. Even if I have to tie her to a chair," he promised.

"You don't have to go to those drastic measures," she told him. But secretly, the thought of knowing that Maisie would be unable to suddenly pop up and ruin their evening was rather appealing, not to mention comforting. "Just make sure she doesn't know where you're going—and with whom."

He looked at her closely. "She really did spook you, didn't she?"

Susan was going to say no, because that sounded braver, but it was also a lie. So she shrugged, trying her best to look casual. "Let's just say I'm not used to being threatened."

"Don't worry, you won't have to get used to it. It won't happen again," he promised.

There was definitely something of the knight in shining armor about the dusty cattle rancher, Susan thought with a smile, watching him leave.

Chapter 12

"Is it true?"

Wes hadn't heard the door to the sheriff's office open, had been too preoccupied working at his desk to even hear anyone come in.

Only in office for a little more than a year and it was already looking as if every unaccounted-for piece of paper in the county had somehow found its way to his desk, presumably to die. A man had to have access to a thirty-hour day—without any sleep—in order to do this job properly and still take care of all this annoying paperwork, he thought darkly.

Right about now, Wes was convinced that he would welcome any distraction to take him away from these damn reports he needed to file. But when he looked up to see his sister standing before his desk, looking every bit like a commercial seeking pledges of money for food for a starving third-world country, he wasn't quite so sure about welcoming *any* distraction.

Maisie, at forty, was his older sister—as well as his only sister—but there were a lot of times when he felt as if he were the older one, not Maisie. These days there was something of the waif about her. Seeing her like that usually brought out his protective instincts.

But dealing with Maisie took a great deal of patience, which in turn meant a great deal of time, and time was something he was rather short on right now. As sheriff of Honey Creek he had a murder with a twist on his hands and the sooner he got to the bottom of it, the sooner life in this small town would go back to normal. Back to people engaging in harmless gossip instead of looking at one another with suspicion and uneasiness. Too many people were heading to the hardware store to buy deadbolts for their doors, something that had been, heretofore, unheard of in Honey Creek.

Maisie's thin but still beautiful face was now a mask of consternation. Wes couldn't even begin to guess why.

His first thought was that whatever had brought her here to him might have something to do with her son, his nephew Jeremy. Or maybe with their father.

And just possibly, both.

His guess turned out to be wrong.

"Is what true?" he finally asked her when she didn't elaborate.

Maisie drew in a shaky breath, as if that would somehow help her push out the next words she needed to say. "Is it true that Mark Walsh came back from the dead?"

That pulled him up short. Where the hell had that come from? There just seemed to be no end to the annoyances this dead man could stir up. "Who told you that?"

Her thin shoulders scratched the air in a hapless shrug. "I heard talk. They said that you found Mark Walsh in the creek." Maisie paused, clearly waiting for him to confirm or deny the statement.

Wes folded his hands on top of the opened report on his desk and looked into his older sister's eyes. "I did."

Maisie stifled a strange, hapless little noise. "Then he did come back from the dead."

She began to tremble visibly, her busy fingers going to her lips as if they could help her find the right words to say next. But only small frightened sounds escaped.

Getting up, Wes abandoned the tiresome work that was spread over the surface of his desk. He considered his sister's peace of mind—or what he was about to coax forward—to be far more important than filing something on time.

Rounding his desk, Wes came over to where Maisie was standing and put his arm around her shoulders in an effort to comfort her. Maisie responded to kind voices and a soft touch.

"No, Maisie, Mark Walsh didn't come back from the dead," he told her in a firm, gentle voice.

But it didn't help. She pulled away from him, her aquamarine eyes wide and frightened. "But we buried him. There was a casket and a body and they were buried," she insisted, her voice bordering on hysteria. "Fifteen years ago, they were buried. I *saw* it."

"It was someone else—" Wes began, still patient. His voice was low, soothing. Damn, he wished Duke was here. Duke always seemed to be able to manage her better than the rest of them could.

"Who?" Maisie wanted to know, almost begging to be convinced she was wrong. If she was wrong, if Mark hadn't come back from the dead to haunt her, then the nightmares she was afraid of wouldn't start again, the way they had when Mark was first buried.

"I don't know," Wes told her wearily, "but it wasn't Walsh." He tried talking to her the way he would to anyone else. To a stable person. "I'm having the first body exhumed to try to see if we can determine who it was." No one else had been reported missing at the time, so for now, he still held to his drifter-in-the-wrong-place-at-the-wrong-time theory.

It was obvious that Maisie was desperately trying to come to terms with what had happened. "But that body you found in the creek, that was Mark?"

"Yes, Maisie, that was Mark Walsh."

Just when he thought he'd made her understand, she suddenly challenged him. "How do you know that was Mark Walsh?"

He supposed it was a fair enough question. He did his best to hang onto his patience. "The county medical examiner matched up Walsh's dental records with the man we fished out of the creek."

Maisie blew out another shaky breath, her eyes never leaving her brother. "And he's really dead?"

Wes tried to give her an encouraging smile. "He's really dead."

She still looked fearful, still unable to believe what he was telling her.

"You're sure?" Clutching at his shirt with her damp fingers, she implored him to convince her. "You're really sure it's him? And that he's dead?"

Very gently, he separated her fingers from his shirt. "Maisie, what's this all about?" An uneasy feeling undulated through him. Could his sister have had something to so with Walsh's death? She did seem unhinged at times and there was no way to gauge what was going on in her head.

She didn't answer his question, she just repeated her own. "Are you sure, Wes?" she pressed, enunciating each word.

"I'm sure. There's no mistake this time. It *is* Mark Walsh and he's dead." Still holding her hands in his, Wes looked into her eyes, trying to make sense out of what was going on. "Maisie, why are you so agitated about this?"

"I don't want the nightmares to start again," she said, more to herself or to someone who wasn't in the room than in response to his question. For a moment, Maisie looked as if she was going to cry, but then she raised her head defiantly, as if issuing a challenge to that same nonexistent person. "Not again."

Wes did what he could to reassure her. He really didn't have time for this. "They won't," he promised her. "Everything's going to be fine, Maisie. Just fine. Look, why don't I take you home? You're too upset right now to be alone."

"All right," she agreed docilely, the agitation leaving her as quickly, as suddenly, as it had come. Subdued, she followed him outside to the street like some obedient pet.

About to open the passenger side of his police vehicle for her, Wes happened to look across the street, to the side entrance of Kelley's Cookhouse. He saw Duke walking out of the restaurant and heading toward his truck.

Wes saw his way out.

"C'mon, Maisie," he urged, "I think I just found you a ride home."

His sister looked at him blankly as he took hold of her arm and propelled her down the street. "I thought you said you were taking me home."

"I was, but then I'd have to come back." But Duke didn't, he thought. Duke was going home.

His brother had already started up his truck. Waving, Wes hurriedly put himself directly in Duke's path. The latter was forced to pick up his hand brake again and turn his engine off.

Now what? Duke wondered.

He stuck his head out through the driver's-side window, looking at Wes. "From what I recollect, they issued you a bulletproof vest when you took this job, not a car-proof vest. You got a death wish, Sheriff?"

Wes came around to Duke's side of the cab. "I need you to get Maisie home."

Duke scowled as he looked at his sister. "Maisie." There was no inflection whatsoever in his voice, no way of telling what he was thinking.

"Yeah, Maisie." And then, because he *was* the sheriff, he had to ask. "Something wrong?"

Maybe Duke knew the reason why Maisie seemed

to be on the verge of hysteria this afternoon. Was it really only about the discovery of Mark Walsh's body— something that was upsetting a lot of people—or was there something else going on? And why was Duke looking at their sister that way? Was he missing something?

Duke suppressed an annoyed sigh. He was not about to tell Wes that their sister had threatened Susan. Even if he wasn't the sheriff, Wes would want to know why Maisie was behaving that way. What was going on—or not going on—between him and Susan was nobody's business but his—and maybe Susan's, he added silently. There was no way he was going to talk about it with anyone.

"No, nothing's wrong," Duke said. His eyes shifted toward his sister who was hanging back. "Get in, Maisie," he told her.

Maisie looked a little hesitant; her initial smile when she'd seen Duke had all but vanished. But when Wes opened the passenger-side door for her, she got into the truck's cab docilely.

Securing the door, Wes crossed back around to Duke's side. Once next to his brother, he lowered his voice and said, "Something about my finding Walsh's body in the creek has her spooked." He paused for a second, debating whether to add the last part. But he decided it couldn't hurt. "Go easy on her."

"I have for the last fifteen years," Duke told his brother.

And maybe that was the problem, Duke thought. Maybe he'd gone too easy on Maisie and that had eventually allowed her to slip into a place where he couldn't readily reach her. Maybe if he'd made her behave a little more responsibly, he'd have done them both a favor.

They were going to have a little talk, he and Maisie, and get things straightened out, Duke promised himself. Once and for all.

Duke started up his truck again and pulled away without saying another word to Wes.

"You don't have to worry about Maisie anymore," Duke told Susan that evening when she opened the door to admit him to her home. A man who believed in getting down to business, he'd skipped a mundane greeting in favor of setting her mind at ease as he walked into the Kelley guest house.

Susan did her best to look composed and nonchalant—not like someone who'd spent the last forty-five minutes two steps away from the front door waiting for Duke to finally arrive.

Duke wasn't late, she was just very early. "Oh?" That came out sounding a little too high, she upbraided herself as she closed the door behind him. He could probably tell she was nervous.

Duke looked around the living room. The house was neat, tidy, with sleek, simple lines. With just enough frills to make him think of her. But then he'd noticed that, lately, a lot of things made him think of her.

"Yeah," he responded. "I had a talk with Maisie." He'd used the time it took him to get his sister back to the main house to his advantage. And Maisie had listened solemnly—and crossed her heart. "She promised not to bother you anymore."

What a woman said was one thing, what she did was another, Susan thought. But she didn't want to spoil the evening by getting into any kind of a discussion about his sister's possible future behavior. So she offered him a bright smile and pretended that she thought everything was going to be just peachy from then on.

"That's good." She knew she should just drop it here, but there was a part of her that was a fighter. That didn't just lie down and wait for the steam roller to come by and finish the job. So she said, "Does that mean she'll stop leaving dead flowers and nasty notes too?"

He looked at her sharply. "You got more?"

She pressed her lips together and nodded. "I got more."

Damn it, who the hell was stalking her? He didn't like thinking that she could be in danger. This was Honey Creek. Things like this didn't happen here—until they did, he thought darkly. Like with Walsh.

"Well, they're not from Maisie," he told her, measuring his words slowly. "I took her home from town and left her sleeping in her room. Jeremy's looking after her," he added.

Though no one would have guessed it, he couldn't help feeling sorry for his nephew. The poor kid had been dealt one hell of a hand. No father, a mother who was only half there mentally and a grandfather whose dislike for the boy was all but tangible whenever the two were in the same room together.

He and his brothers did what they could to make Jeremy feel that he was part of the family, but it wasn't easy when Darius was just as determined to make

Jeremy feel like an outsider subsisting solely on the old man's charity.

"Anyone else in my family you think is sending them?" he asked her archly.

She bristled slightly. "I didn't mean to sound as if I was focusing on your family," she apologized. "But this has me a little shaken up. There's no reason for *anyone* to be sending me dead roses and threatening notes, but they still keep on coming."

He heard the distress in her voice, even though she struggled to hide just how nervous this was making her. Nobody was going to hurt her if he had anything to say about it.

"For my money I still think it's that Hayes character," he told her, then repeated his offer. "You want me to talk to him?"

She shook her head. "It's not Linc. He wouldn't do something like this." She was certain of it. They were friends, good friends. He wouldn't resort to this kind of mental torture.

Duke didn't quite see it that way. " 'Fraid you've got a lot more faith in Hayes than I do. Let me take the latest note and the last batch of flowers with me when I leave. I'll bring them over to Wes tomorrow, see if he's gotten anywhere with his investigation."

Susan wondered if he realized the significance of his offer. In case the small detail eluded him, she pointed it out. "That means you'll have to admit to seeing me. Are you ready to do that?"

Duke knew a challenge when he saw one. And Susan, whether she knew it or not, was definitely challenging him. Calling him out.

"Woman, I've been on my own for a lot of years," he told her. "I don't have to ask anyone's permission to do anything I want to do." He left the rest unsaid and let her fill in the blanks.

"What about your father?" she asked. "Don't you have to run things by him?"

She'd heard that the patriarch of the Colton clan could make life a living hell for anyone who crossed him. He was a strict man who demanded allegiance and obedience from the people he dealt with, especially from his own family.

"Only when it comes to things that concern the ranch," he allowed. And there was a reason for that. "The ranch is his. My life is mine. Any other questions or things you'd like to clear up?"

She had to admit she felt a little more at ease. Susan smiled at him. "Can't think of a thing."

"All right, then let's go," he prodded. It was getting late and he'd promised her dinner in town. When she made no move to follow him out the door, Duke raised one eyebrow. "Change your mind?"

"Only about where we're eating," she replied. He raised his eyebrow even higher. "I thought maybe we could eat in. I threw some things together," she explained, then stopped, wondering if maybe she was taking too much for granted or sending out the wrong signals again. This creating a relationship was hard work. Worth it, but hard work.

Duke asked, "Edible things?"

He was teasing her. Susan didn't bother attempting to hide her smile. She considered herself a very good cook, having inherited her father's natural instincts for creating epicurean miracles.

"Very."

That was good enough for him. Duke took his hat off and let it fall onto the cushion of the wide, padded leather sofa to his right.

"Talked me into it," he told her.

His eyes caught hers. He felt something stirring inside him. Anticipation. It surprised him and he savored it for a moment. In so many ways, Charlene had been superior to Susan. Experienced, clever and worldly, she'd been a woman in every sense of the word. And yet, there was something about Susan, something that pulled him to her, that had him looking forward to being with her, more than he'd *ever* looked forward to being with Charlene. Who would have thought—?

"This way," he continued pointedly, "we won't have to go so far or wait so long for dessert."

Dessert. Was that what he was calling it? Or was she reading too much into his words? Too much because she desperately wanted him to mean that he wanted her. Wanted to believe that he had planned the evening around dinner and lovemaking.

Because she'd thought of nothing else since he'd asked her about her plans when he came to her office earlier today.

"Come this way," she invited. Turning on her heel, she led him into her small dining room.

Duke entertained himself by watching the way Susan's trim hips moved as she walked ahead of him. It reminded him of a prize show pony he'd once owned, a gift from his grandfather when he'd been a young boy.

The pony had had the same classy lines, the same proud gait as Susan did now. It had been a thing of beauty to watch when it ran, he recalled.

Just like Susan was a thing of beauty to behold when she was in his arms. Making love with him.

Wow.

He hadn't realized he was even capable of having thoughts like that. Susan was definitely bringing out the best in him, he mused. Making him want to be a better man. For her.

He found himself hoping she hadn't made very much for dinner because whatever was on the table wasn't going to whet his appetite one-tenth as much as the taste of her mouth would.

And that was what he craved right now. Her. But she'd gone to all this trouble, it wasn't right to ask her to skip it because he was having trouble holding back his more basic appetites.

"Sit down," she told him. "This won't take long, I promise."

"Need any help?" he offered, raising his voice so that it would carry into the kitchen.

Her back to him, Susan's mouth curved in pure pleasure. She would never have believed that Duke Colton would actually offer to help out in the kitchen. As a matter of fact, she would have been fairly certain that Duke didn't even know what to do in a kitchen. You just never knew, did you?

"No, everything's fine," she answered, tossing the words over her shoulder. "All you have to do is sit there and enjoy yourself."

Susan's casual instruction brought an actual grin to Duke's lips before he could think to stop it.

He fully intended to, he thought. He fully intended to.

Marie Ferrarella

the looks Bonnie Gene
and had been giving her each time
They may not be pretty, but they keep

Chapter 13

Susan sighed.

She finally put down her pen and gave up her flimsy pretense that she hadn't noticed the looks Bonnie Gene had been giving her each time the woman walked by the open office door. Which was frequently this morning. Susan had lost count at eleven.

"All right, Mother, what is it?"

Bonnie Gene had already gone by and had to backtrack her steps in order to present herself in the doorway.

"What's what, dear?" her mother asked innocently.

The stage had lost one hell of a performer when her mother had decided not to pursue an acting career, Susan thought.

"You know perfectly well 'what's what,'" Susan insisted. "You must have walked by my office about a dozen times this morning. And each time, you looked in with that self-satisfied smile of yours." When her mother raised a quizzical eyebrow, Susan continued to elaborate. "You know, the one you always wear whenever you place first in the annual pie-baking contest."

"I *always* place first in the pie-baking contest," Bonnie Gene informed her regally. "Unless the judges were being bribed that year or had their taste buds surgically removed."

Susan stopped her mother before she could get carried away. "Don't change the subject."

Another innocent look graced Bonnie Gene's face as she placed a hand delicately against her still very firm bosom. "I thought that was the subject."

Okay, Susan thought, *we could go around like this indefinitely.* She worded her question more precisely. "Mother, why do you keep looking in at me?"

Bonnie Gene crossed the threshold, her smile rivaling the summer sun outside. "Because you're my lovely daughter—"

"Mother!" Susan cried far more sharply than she would have ordinarily, impatience shimmering around the single name. "Come clean. What's going on?"

Bonnie Gene adopted a more serious demeanor. "I should be asking you that."

"You could," Susan allowed, feeling her patience being stripped away. "*If* you explained what you meant by your question."

"Don't play innocent with me, my darling." Bonnie Gene looked at her daughter pointedly, having lingered on the word *innocent* a beat longer than the rest of her sentence. "The time for that is past, thank goodness. All right, all right," she declared, giving up the last shred of pretense as Susan began to get up from her chair. "I can't stand not knowing any longer."

"Not knowing *what?*" Susan cried, completely frustrated. What was it that her mother was carrying on about? It couldn't possibly be about her and—

"How things are going with you and Duke Colton."

Oh, God, it was *about her and Duke.*

In response, Susan turned a lighter shade of pale and sank back down in her chair. She'd been afraid of this.

"What are you talking about?" she finally asked in a small, still, disembodied voice that didn't seem to belong to her.

With a superior air, one hand fisted at her hip, Bonnie Gene tossed her head, sending her hair flying jauntily over her shoulder. "Oh, come now, Susan, you didn't *really* think that you could keep this to yourself, did you?"

In retrospect, Susan supposed that had been pretty stupid of her. Her mother had eyes like a hawk and the sensory perception of a bat; all in all, a pretty frightening combination. Especially since it meant that *nothing* ever seemed to escape her attention.

"I had hopes," Susan murmured, almost to herself. She raised her eyes and blew out a breath, bracing herself for the answer to the question she was about to ask. "Who else knows?"

Bonnie Gene laughed. She staked out a place for herself on the corner of Susan's desk and leaned over to be closer to her youngest.

"An easier question to answer, my love, is who else

doesn't know. I must say though, I've had my work cut out for me."

"Your work?" Susan echoed, really lost this time. What was her mother talking about now?

"Yes." Bonnie Gene looked at Susan as if completely surprised that she didn't understand. "Defending your choice. Defending *Duke*," she finally stressed.

"There is no 'choice,' Mother," Susan informed Bonnie Gene, knowing that she really didn't have a leg to stand on. She *had* chosen Duke. The problem was, as of yet, she had no idea how the man really felt about her. There were no terms of endearment coming from him, no little gifts now that she had ruled out that those awful flowers had been from him.

For all she knew, Duke was just seeing her because he had no one better within easy access at the moment. She knew that making herself available to him if she believed that made her seem like a pathetic woman, but she couldn't help it. She was so very attracted to Duke, she would accept him on almost any terms as long as it meant that the evening would end with them sharing passion. When she was away from him, she was counting off minutes in her head until they were together again.

But that was by no means something she wanted her mother—or anyone else for that matter—to know. At least, not until she knew how Duke felt about her.

And for that matter, maybe it was better that she didn't know how he felt. She was more than a little aware that the truth could be very painful.

"And exactly what do you mean *defending Duke?*"

Susan suddenly asked, replaying her mother's words in her head.

Bonnie Gene rolled her eyes dramatically. "Well, I can't begin to tell you how many people have come up to me, wanting to know what a nice girl like you is doing with a man the likes of Duke Colton. If I hear one more 'concerned' citizen tell me about Charlene's suicide after Duke broke it off with her, I'll scream—if I don't throw up first."

Susan squared her shoulders, indignation shining in her eyes. She resented the gossipmongers having a field day with Duke's past behavior, and they were all missing a very salient point.

"Duke broke it off with Charlene when he found out she was married. He told me that he would have never been involved with her in the first place if he'd known that she wasn't single." In her eyes, he had done the right thing, the honorable thing. Why couldn't anyone else see that?

"Simmer down, Susan, I believe you." Bonnie Gene smiled into her daughter's face, lightly touching the hair that framed it. "As much as I want to see you married, I wouldn't let you throw your life away on someone I didn't think was good enough for you. What kind of a mother would that make me, if all I wanted was just to get you married off?" She looked at her daughter pointedly.

She was right, Susan thought. There were times that she forgot that, at bottom, her mother loved and cared about all of them. Worried about all of them. She'd lost sight of that amid all the less than veiled hints that came trippingly off Bonnie Gene's tongue about time running out.

"Sorry," Susan said quietly.

Bonnie Gene beamed, looking more like her older sister than her mother. "Apology accepted. Now," she drew in closer, her eyes lively and hopeful, "how *is* it going between the two of you?"

Her mother deserved the truth, Susan thought. "I don't know," Susan confessed. "It's a little early to tell. We've only been seeing each other for two weeks," Susan pointed out, using the innocent phrase *seeing each other* as a euphemism for what was really going on: that they had been making pulse-racing, exquisite love for those two weeks.

In truth, she felt as if she was living in a dream. But dreams, Susan knew, had a terrible habit of ending, forcing the dreamer to wake up. She dreaded the thought of that coming to pass and could only hope that it wouldn't happen too soon. She'd never felt like this before, as if she could just fly at will and touch the sky, gathering stars.

"Time isn't a factor. I knew the first time your father kissed me," Bonnie Gene told her with pride. She saw the skeptical expression that descended over the girl's face. "Oh, I know what you're thinking—your father is this overly round man with an unruly gray mane and a gravelly voice, but he didn't always look like that."

Bonnie Gene closed her eyes for a moment, remembering. The sigh that escaped was pregnant with memories.

"When I first met your father, he was beautiful. And what that man could do—" Bonnie Gene stopped abruptly, realizing who she was talking to. Clearing her throat, she waved her hand dismissively. "Well, never mind. The point is, it doesn't take months to know if you want to spend the rest of your life with someone or not. It just takes a magic moment."

That rang true. For her. For Duke, not so much. "Well, as far as I know, Duke hasn't had a magic moment," Susan told her.

Bonnie Gene heard what wasn't being said. "But you have." It wasn't a question.

Susan didn't want to go on record with that. "Mother, if I don't get back to putting together a spectacular menu, Shirley and Bill Nelson are going to let her sister take over cooking for the party," she protested. "And I don't want that to happen."

Bonnie Gene leaned even further over the desk and lightly kissed the top of her daughter's head. "Go, work. Make your father proud. I have what I wanted to know," she assured Susan.

"Mother." There was a note of pleading in Susan's voice.

Bonnie Gene smiled. "My lips are sealed."

Susan sincerely doubted that.

"Only if you get run over by a sewing machine between here and the kitchen," Susan murmured. No one would have ever recruited Bonnie Gene to be a spy whose ability to keep secrets meant the difference between life and death in the free world.

Bonnie Gene stuck her head in one last time. "I heard that."

"Good, you were supposed to."

Susan attempted to get back to work. She really did

need to finish this menu today. *Something exciting that isn't expensive*—those had been Shirley Nelson's instructions. So far, she really hadn't come up with anything outstanding.

Her ability to concentrate was derailed the next moment as she heard her mother all but purr the words, "Oh, how nice to see you again," to someone outside her door, then adding, "Yes, you're in luck. She's in her office."

The next second, Susan heard a quick rap on her doorjamb. She didn't have to ask who it was because he was there, filling up her doorway and her heart at the same time.

And looking far more appealingly rugged and handsome than any man had a legal right to be.

"Hi," Duke said, his deep voice rumbling at her, creating tidal waves inside her stomach and an instant yearning within the rest of her.

"Hi," Susan echoed back.

"I just ran into your mother," Duke told her needlessly.

He was at a loss as to how to initiate a conversation with Susan, even at this point. Coming to see a woman was new for him. Usually, the women would come seeking him out, their agendas clearly mapped out in their eyes. Conversation had very little to do with it. This was virgin territory he was treading—appropriately enough, he added to himself as an afterthought.

The thought hit him again that he had been Susan's first. He couldn't really say that had ever mattered to him before, but this time around was different. He realized that he liked being her first.

Her only, at least for now.

Even though it brought with it a rather heavy sense of responsibility he'd never felt before. A heavy sense of responsibility not because of anything that Susan had said or demanded, but just because he felt it.

"Yes, I heard," Susan answered.

The first few moments were still awkward between them every time they met and she couldn't even explain why. It wasn't as if they hadn't seen each other for a while. Duke had come over just last night. As he had every other night since the first time they had made love. The time they spent pretending that they intended to go somewhere or do something had been growing progressively shorter. They were in each other's arms, enjoying one another, enjoying lovemaking, faster with each day that passed by.

What pleased her almost as much was that he did talk to her once the lovemaking was over. Talked to her about little things, like what he'd done at the ranch that day, or his plans for a herd of his own. It meant the world to her.

Please don't let it end yet. Not yet, she prayed, watching him walk into the room.

Out loud, she asked, "Um, can I get you anything?"

The hint of a wicked little smile touched the corners of his mouth, sending yet another ripple through her stomach.

"Not here," he told her.

To anyone else, it might have sounded like an enigmatic response, but she knew exactly what he was saying to her. And it thrilled her. She had absolutely no idea where any of this was headed, or even if it was headed anywhere, but she knew she was determined to enjoy every moment of this relationship for as long as it lasted.

Susan was well aware that in comparison to the other women Duke had been with, she could be seen as naive and completely unworldly. Consequently, she wasn't about to fool herself into thinking that she and Duke actually had some kind of a future together. Not in this world any way, she thought. He wasn't the marrying kind. Everyone knew that.

She blushed a little at his response and heard Duke laugh as he crooked his finger beneath her chin and raised her head until her eyes met his.

Damn, but there was something about her, something that just kept on pulling him in, he thought, watching the pink hue on her cheeks begin to fade again. Each time he made love with her, he expected that was finally going to be that. That he'd reached the end of the line.

But he hadn't.

He hadn't had his fill of her, wasn't growing tired of her. He wasn't even aching for his freedom the way he normally did whenever something took up his time to this extent.

Maybe it was a bug going round, he reasoned, searching for something to blame, to explain away his odd behavior satisfactorily.

"I just came by to let you know that I'm going to be late coming by your place tonight," he told her. "I'm in town to pick up some extra supplies and what I'm doing's going to take more time than I thought."

Susan nodded, thrilling to his slightest touch. And

to the promise of the evening that was yet to come. She didn't care how late he came, as long as he came.

"I'll keep a candle burning in the window for you," she promised.

Why did the silly little things she said make him want to smile? And why did she seem to fill up so much of his thoughts, even when he should be thinking of something else?

If he didn't watch out, he was going to get sloppy and careless. And then he'd have his father on his back, watching him like a hawk. That was all he needed. He could guarantee that a blow-up would follow.

"You do that," he told Susan.

Still holding his finger beneath her chin, he bent his head and brushed his lips quickly over hers.

Her eyes fluttered shut as she absorbed the fleeting contact and reveled in it. She could feel her pulse accelerating.

When she opened her eyes, she found him looking at her. More than anything, she wished she could read his thoughts.

"Um, listen, since you're here, can I get you something to eat?" she wanted to know. "It's almost lunch time and I'm assuming that your father lets you have time off for good behavior."

The smallest whisper of a smile played along Duke's lips. She ached to kiss him again, but managed to restrain herself.

"Who says I have good behavior?" he asked. His voice sounded almost playful—for Duke. It sent more ripples through her, reinforcing the huge tidal wave that had washed over her when he'd kissed her.

"No, really," she tried to sound more serious. "Aren't you hungry?" She nodded in the general direction of the kitchen. "I could just whip up something quick for you—"

Yes, he was hungry he thought, but the consumption of food had nothing to do with it. He wanted her. A lot. Another first, he realized.

"If I stay to eat," he told her, his eyes holding hers, "I might not leave anytime soon."

They weren't talking about food. Even she knew that. And the idea that she could actually entice someone like Duke Colton thrilled her beyond measure.

"Wouldn't want to do that."

Her words were agreeing with him, her tone was not. Her tone told him that she wanted nothing more than to have him stay and do all those wondrous things to her that he had introduced her to. Just the thought of it stirred his appetite.

He looked at her for a long moment, debating. The door had a lock on it.

"Oh, I don't know about that," he answered speculatively, allowing his voice to trail off.

But the thought of being interrupted by one of the staff, or either of her parents, tipped the scales toward behaving more sensibly. He told himself that passing up a chance to make love with her now meant that there was more to look forward to tonight.

Suppressing a sigh, Duke gathered himself together and crossed to the doorway. He nodded his head. "See you tonight."

"Tonight," she echoed to his retreating back.

Tonight.

The single world throbbed with promise. If she weren't afraid of her mother passing by again and looking in, she would have hugged herself.

Chapter 14

The extra feed he'd come for all loaded up in his truck, Duke got behind the wheel, put his key into the ignition and turned it on.

Then he turned it off again.

He'd never been a man given to impulsive moves. He thought things through before he did them. But he was here, so he took advantage of time and opportunity. Taking the note that Susan had given him, he got out of the truck's cab, secured the door and went to the short, squat building across the street.

Wes's car was parked outside. That meant that Wes was most likely inside or close by. Duke walked into the sheriff's office without bothering to knock. He was a man with a timetable.

"I know you're busy with looking into Mark Walsh's latest murder, but I really need you to look into this for me," he declared, holding the crudely handwritten note out in front of him. "Susan got another one. Along with more dead flowers."

About to leave to grab some lunch, Wes took a step backward in order to allow his older brother to come in. Taking the note that Duke held out to him, he glanced at it quickly. Same block letters, an equally childish threat on the sheet.

"You mean you want me to look into this in my spare time between midnight and 12:04 a.m.?" he asked wryly. He wasn't a man who complained, but venting a little steam wasn't entirely out of order. He'd been hunting for Walsh's killer even before the autopsy had confirmed his identity—and getting nowhere. "I had no idea there were so many people who hated Mark Walsh." Wes walked back to his desk and sat down, placing the note on top of the pile of papers that were there. "Right now, the only ones who I know aren't suspects are Damien and me."

Hooking his thumbs onto his belt, Duke continued to stand, his countenance all but shouting that he was a man with things to do, places to go. "That bad?"

"Pretty much. Hell, the spooked way Maisie's been acting lately, if I didn't know any better, I'd say that she did the guy in herself." Wes rocked back in his chair, glancing again at the note that Duke had brought in. He'd hoped that the previous notes and flowers had been a prank that had played itself out. Obviously not, he thought. "I'm starting to think that maybe getting elected sheriff was not the wisest career move I could have made."

Duke had never seen the appeal of the position, but

he'd backed Wes's choice nonetheless. "Still better than ranching with the old man."

"You do have a point." Straightening up, Wes frowned as he perused the note more closely. "Now, remind me again what is it I'm looking for?" he asked, *other than a little sleep,* he added silently.

"Find out who sent the notes and the flowers," Duke replied simply.

Wes raised a quizzical eyebrow. "This is important to you, isn't it?"

Duke was about to say no, that it was all one and the same to him, but it was upsetting Susan, but that would have been a lie and Wes had a knack of seeing through lies.

Maybe he shouldn't have come here, pushing the issue, Duke thought. He didn't want Wes picking through his business. But then, this wasn't about him, it was about Susan, about her safety. He was beginning to get worried that maybe whoever was sending these notes and the dead flowers wasn't exactly up for the most sane person of the year award. If that person turned out to be dangerous as well…

He shrugged. "She's afraid. I don't like seeing women threatened."

Wes looked at him knowingly. "You seeing Susan Kelley?" It wasn't really so much a question as it was a statement seeking verification.

Duke managed to tamp down his startled surprise. "What makes you say that?" he asked in a toneless voice.

"Because I'm a brilliant detective, because I've got fantastic gut instincts—" and then he gave Duke the real reason "—and because Maisie complained to me that you're going to ruin the family line by getting the Kelley girl pregnant."

Damn it, he thought Maisie and he had settled this. Apparently he needed to have another talk with her, Duke thought, annoyed. Out loud, he confirmed Wes's guess. "Yeah, maybe I'm seeing her."

"Either you are, or you're not," Wes pointed out, looking at him, waiting for an answer.

"Okay, I am. For now," he qualified, leaving himself a way out. "Now, are you going to look into this for her sometime before the turn of the next century?" he asked irritably. "Someone's been leaving these on her doorstep the last couple of weeks, along with bunches of dead flowers," he reiterated, in case Wes had forgotten.

"And you really don't have any idea who's been doing this?"

Duke looked down at his brother pointedly. "I wouldn't be talking to you if I did."

"Good point, although I'd rather not have one of my brothers turn vigilante on me. Especially not now when we're finally getting Damien out." He figured there was nothing wrong with issuing a veiled warning to his brother. If it didn't come out in so many words, there was more of a chance of Duke complying with it.

A cynical smile touched the corners of Duke's mouth. "When she first started getting them, Susan really thought that I was the one sending them."

Wes surprised him by nodding. "I can see why she might." Duke looked at him sharply. "You're so damn closed-mouthed, nobody ever knows what's going on in that head of yours. You're like this big, black cloud on the horizon. Nobody can make an intelligent guess if it's going to rain or just pass through. And you're always frowning. Hell, when I was a kid, I thought that scowl of yours was set in stone."

Duke blew out an impatient sigh. "I don't have time for memory lane, Wes. Just take a few hours away from the Walsh thing and look into this for me, okay?" He couldn't remember when he'd asked Wes for something, so he took it for granted that Wes's response would be in the affirmative.

He wasn't prepared for the slightly amused grin that curved his brother's mouth.

"What?" Duke demanded.

"You and Susan Kelley, huh?"

Duke's eyes narrowed to small, dark slits. "That is none of your business."

Wes would have been lying if he hadn't admitted that contradicting Duke stirred up more than a small amount of satisfaction. "Well, actually, with my being sheriff, it kinda is if for some reason the two of you being together made someone write these." He nodded at the note on his desk for emphasis. "And if we're talking personal—"

"We're not," Duke quickly bit off.

Wes ignored Duke's disclaimer and continued with his thought. "I think it's great that you've finally moved on and put that whole Charlene McWilliams thing behind you. Susan looks like a really great girl—and she's just what you need."

Duke was not about to admit anything, even if, somewhere in his soul, he secretly agreed with his brother's pronouncement. That was his business, not anyone else's. Just like he felt something lighting up inside of him every time he saw Susan was his business.

"I wasn't aware that I needed anything," Duke said, his voice a monotone.

"That just means that you need it more than the rest of us," Wes told him with a knowing smile. "Not a single one of the Almighty's creatures does better without love than with it."

Annoyed, Duke asked him with more than a small touch of sarcasm, "You thinking of becoming a philosopher now, too?"

Wes took no offense. He hadn't expected Duke to suddenly profess how he felt about the girl. Duke had trouble coming to grips with feelings, they all knew that.

"No, just happy someday, if the right woman crosses my path," Wes qualified.

Duke sighed and shook his head. He was not about to get into a discussion over this. "Just get back to me on that," he instructed, nodding at the note.

Wes rose and walked with his brother to the door. "Don't let that bit about being 'a servant of the people' fool you, big brother. Just so we're clear, I find this guy, *I'll* handle it, not you." There was no negotiation on this point.

Though he wouldn't say it in so many words, Duke gave his younger brother his due. "Whatever," he muttered as he walked out.

"Nice talking to you too, big brother," Wes said to Duke's back.

The phone in Susan's office rang as she got up to walk out for the evening. She looked longingly toward the doorway.

It wasn't like her to ignore a call. Susan was one of those people who felt a compulsion to answer every phone that rang, whenever it rang. But she knew that if she picked up this time, she'd wind up leaving the office and town later than she wanted to.

She didn't want to have to amend her schedule. What she wanted to do was hurry home and get ready for her evening with Duke. Granted there was nothing special planned—just being together was special enough as far as she was concerned—but she wanted to take her time getting ready tonight. That meant actually indulging in a bubble bath for a decadent twenty minutes—fifteen minutes longer than she usually spent in the shower.

And there was this new scent she wanted to try out, something that she had ordered via the Internet and that smelled like sin in a bottle. She was anxious to wear something as different as possible from her usual cologne whose light scent brought fresh roses to mind. After being on the receiving end of all those dead roses, roses were the last thing she wanted wafting around her as she moved about.

Susan had almost made it out of the office when she finally stopped. Guilt got the better of her.

Turning around, she hurried back to her desk and picked up the receiver just as her answering machine clicked on.

"This is Susan," she told the caller, raising her voice above the recorded greeting. "Wait until the tape in the answering machine stops before talking."

But her instructions came too late. Whoever was on the other end of the line had hung up.

Well, she'd tried, she thought, replacing the receiver

into its cradle. At least this way, she told herself silently, she didn't have to feel guilty.

Guilt was the last emotion she wanted lingering around when Duke was with her.

Glancing one last time at the package she was bringing home with her—she'd made beef tenderloin with a green chili and garlic sauce as well as a double serving of grilled vegetables for dinner tonight—she smiled and hurried out.

The dinner's warm, welcoming aroma followed her to her car and then filled up the space around her as she closed the door. Susan started up her car.

Ultimately, this aroma would probably tempt Duke more than the expensive perfume she just bought would, she thought.

But she hoped not.

Reaching home, she parked her car, grabbed her package and raced inside. It struck her, as she closed the door behind her, that she'd left it unlocked again. She was forever forgetting to lock the door when she left in the morning. But this was Honey Creek, she reasoned. Other than Mark Walsh's death—and those stupid notes along with the dead flowers—nothing ever happened here. It was a nice, safe little town.

Hurrying, she took the warming tray out of the cabinet and got it ready to be pressed into service once she finished her bubble bath. She put the package on the counter beside the tray and raced off to the bathroom.

Too excited to come close to relaxing, Susan shaved six minutes off her bubble bath and utilized that extra time fixing her hair and makeup.

She'd decided to show Duke that she wasn't just another fresh-scrubbed face. That she could be pretty—maybe even more than a tad pretty—if she set her mind to it, given the right "tools."

So she carefully applied the mini battalion of shadows, mascara and highlighters she'd amassed and redid her hair three times before she was ultimately satisfied with the woman she saw looking back at her from the mirror.

Throwing on a light-blue, ankle-length robe to protect the shimmery royal-blue dress that only went half way down her shapely thighs, Susan hurried back to the kitchen. She wanted to do a few last-minute things to the dinner so she could put the meal out of her mind until it was time to serve it.

Just as she entered the kitchen, Susan could have sworn she saw something hurry past the large window located over the double sink.

Probably just some stray animal, lost, she decided, and looking to find its way back.

Aren't we all? she mused, grinning.

It wasn't unheard of to catch a glimpse of a stray deer every so often, although now that she thought about it, there'd been fewer sightings in the last couple of years.

That was the price of progress, a trade-off. Two-legged creatures instead of four-legged ones.

Plugging in the warming tray, she froze, listening. She was certain she'd heard a noise coming from the front of the house.

It *wasn't* her imagination. She *had* heard something.

Her parents—even her mother—didn't just come over without either calling first or at the very least, ringing the doorbell to give her half a second's warning before they walked in.

And she *knew* that Duke wouldn't play games like this, making noise to scare her. The man didn't play games at all.

Grabbing a twelve-inch carving knife out of the wooden block that held the set of pearl-handled knives that her mother had given her for her catering business, Susan tightly wrapped her fingers around it.

"Is anyone there?" she called out.

Susan thought of the gun her father had tried to convince her into taking when she had moved in here. She wished now that she hadn't been so stubborn about it. A gun would have made her feel more in control of the situation.

It was probably nothing, she told herself as she inched toward the front of the house. Just the wind causing one of the larger tree branches to bang against the living-room bay window.

It was the last thing to cross her mind before the searing pain exploded at the back of her skull.

The next moment, everything went black.

Susan dreamt she was drowning. She struggled to reach the surface and gulp in air. It took her a beat to realize that she wasn't in the creek, desperately trying to swim for the bank while Mark Walsh tried to pull her back under. She was in her house.

And then she gasped, trying to breathe. Someone

had just thrown water in her face. A lot of water, all at once.

Coughing and gasping, it took her another couple of beats before she became completely aware of her surroundings.

She *was* still in her house, in the kitchen. But instead of standing by the counter, she was sitting on a chair. Not just sitting but sealed onto it. Duct tape all but cocooned her waist and thighs, holding her fast against the wood. Her hands were bound behind her. She couldn't move no matter how hard she pulled against the silvery tape.

Afraid, wild-eyed, Susan looked around, trying to understand what was going on. Her head felt as if it was splitting in half, the pain radiating from the back of her skull to the front.

She couldn't see anyone but she *knew* that there was someone in the house with her. Someone who had hit her from behind and then bound her up like an Egyptian mummy. But who could have done this?

Maisie?

Linc?

And if not either of them, then who? And why?

Her thoughts collided as she struggled to control the hysteria that threatened to overwhelm her.

"Who's there?" she cried. "Why are you doing this? Show yourself," she demanded, doing her best to sound angry and not as afraid as she really was. "Show yourself so we can talk. You don't want to do this."

She heard someone moving behind her and tried to turn her head as far as she could in that direction. But she needn't have bothered. The person who had put her in this position moved into her line of vision.

"Oh, but I do," the thin-framed, weatherbeaten, nondescript man told her. "You can't even *begin* to understand how much I want to do this."

Susan stared at the man. He was maybe as tall as she was, maybe shorter. She didn't know him. His face meant nothing to her and no name came to mind. No frame of reference suggested itself.

Why did he hate her?

"Why?" she managed to ask hoarsely, fear all but closing up her throat. "Why do you want to tie me up like this?"

"I don't want to tie you up," he informed her condescendingly. "That's just a means to an end." He brought his face in close to hers. The man reeked of whiskey. Had he worked himself up, seeking courage in a bottle before going on this rampage? "I want to hurt you," he said, enunciating each word. "I want to make you slowly bleed out your life, just like she did."

This was a mistake. It had to be a mistake. She needed to get this man to talk, to make him see that what he was doing was crazy.

If nothing else, she needed to stall him. To stall him until Duke came to save her from this maniac.

"Like who did?" she asked urgently. "Who are you talking about?"

His face contorted, as if someone had just hit him in the gut and the pain was almost too much to bear. "My wife. My wife killed herself because that worthless scum you're playing whore for walked out on her." Again he stuck his face into hers. "Do you know how that feels?" he demanded. "Do you have *any* idea how it feels to know that your wife would rather kill herself than come back to you?"

He straightened up, reliving the memory in his mind. Staring off into space, he sucked in a long, ragged breath.

"I thought my gut had been ripped out when I had to go and identify her body. They found her in her car, her wrists slashed." There were angry tears shimmering in his eyes. The next second, the tears were replaced with rage. "Well, that's what I want Duke Colton to feel. I want him to feel like he's been gutted when he looks at what I've left behind for him."

Picking up the knife that she had dropped when he'd knocked her unconscious, Hank McWilliams held it for a moment, as if contemplating the would-be weapon's weight and feel.

A strange look came into his eyes as he looked back at her. "Had a notion to become a doctor once. Studied on my own. Didn't matter, though. Never got to be a doctor because there weren't enough money." The smile that slipped across his lips made her blood run cold. "But I know where every vital organ is. And I know how and where to cut a man so that he stays alive for a very long, long time." His smugness increased. "Same goes for a woman," he concluded, delivering the first cut so quickly, she didn't even see it coming.

Susan heard the shrill, bloody scream and realized belatedly that it was coming from her.

The next second she felt the sting of his hand as he slapped her across the face.

"Damn it, whore," he exclaimed, then seemed to

regain control over himself. "My fault," he mumbled under his breath. "Forgot that you'd scream."

Leaving the knife on the floor for a second, McWilliams ripped off an oversize piece of duct tape and clamped it hard over her mouth. He smoothed it down over and over again to make sure it stayed in place.

"That should keep you quiet," he announced, deftly slicing her two more times in her chest and abdomen. As the blood began to flow, he laughed gleefully, his eyes bright and dancing. "This might go quicker than I thought," he told her, his tone as unhurried as if he was timing something in the oven instead of watching her life drain from her.

Susan struggled to stay conscious, trying to focus on what time it was. How long had she been out? Where was Duke?

And then she remembered. He'd said he was going to be late tonight.

Fear wrapped itself around her, making it all but impossible to breathe as the blade of the maniac's knife sliced through her flesh as quickly and easily as if she was only a stick of butter.

The duct tape stifled the scream that tore from her throat, defusing it. Susan still screamed for all she was worth, her head spinning wildly from the effort and from the pain.

She was barely hanging on to consciousness by her fingertips.

He slashed into her flesh again, twisting the knife this time.

Chapter 15

Duke had worked at a quick, steady pace all afternoon, taking no breaks, creating shortcuts when he could. Though he told himself he was only being practical and that working this quickly would get him out of the sun faster—a sun that was beating down on him without mercy—he knew that he was just feeding himself a line of bull. That wasn't the real reason he was working this hard and he knew it.

The real reason had soft brown eyes that could melt a man's soul and even softer lips. Lips that made him forget about everything else. Lips that, for the first time in his life, actually made him glad to be alive instead of just feeling as if he was marking time until something of some sort of import happened.

For him, it already had.

He'd met someone he'd known, more or less, for most

of his life. Certainly for all of hers. Someone who, the more he saw her, the more he *wanted* to see her.

Damn, he didn't even know where all these complicated thoughts were suddenly coming from. What was going on with him anyway, Duke scolded himself as he drove up to Susan's house.

Stopping the truck, he took one last look at himself in the rearview mirror, angling it so that he could see if his hair still looked combed or if the hot breeze had ruffled it too much.

He'd taken a quick shower and changed before coming here but still looked sweaty. It had never bothered him before, but now it mattered that he looked his best.

Though he'd never told her, he liked the way Susan ran her fingers through his hair, liked the way she looked up at him, half innocent, half vixen. And when he came right down to it, he didn't know which half he liked better. Was a time he would have known, would have picked vixen hands down.

Now, though...

Tabling his thoughts, he got out of the truck. Duke walked up to Susan's front door and raised his hand to knock.

The sound of a man's voice, coming from within the house, stopped him. There wasn't another car parked in the driveway to give a clue as to who it may be.

That wasn't her father, he thought. The timbre of the voice was all wrong. Donald Kelley had a raspy, coated voice, the kind that came from decades of sipping whiskey on hot, summer nights. This voice belonged to someone else.

To another man.

Duke glanced at his watch. He was early, at least earlier than he'd told her he'd be. Was she "entertaining" someone else while she waited for him?

Well, why the hell not? It wasn't as if any pledges had been made between them. Hell, there wasn't even any wordless understanding. They were both free to do whatever they wanted with whomever they wanted.

Even so, the thought of Susan being with another man angered him more than he thought it would. More than he'd ever felt before.

He glared at the door. He could hear the man talking again.

The hell with her.

He didn't need this, didn't need the aggravation or the humiliation. Turning on his heel, he started to walk away. He was better off giving the whole breed a wide berth, just as he had before he'd gotten roped in by doe eyes and a shy smile.

Shy his as—

Duke's head whipped around toward the door.

Was that a scream? It sounded awfully muffled if it was. But what he had absolutely no doubt about was the streak of fear he'd heard echoing within the suppressed scream.

Making up his mind to go in, he tried the doorknob and found that it wouldn't give. She'd finally learned to lock her door, he thought.

There it was again. A muffled scream, he'd bet his life on it.

Duke's anger gave way to an acute uneasiness, which in turn gave way to fear, even though he couldn't logically have explained why.

Susan was in trouble. His gut told him so.

Instead of calling out to her, Duke braced his right shoulder, tightened his muscles the way he did whenever he lifted one of the heavier bales of hay on his own and slammed his shoulder hard against the door.

It gave only a little.

With a loud grunt that was 50 percent rage and 50 percent fear, Duke slammed his aching shoulder into the door again. As he braced himself for another go-round, he caught a glimpse of Bonnie Gene and Donald coming out of their house and heading in his direction. There was a puzzled look on Bonnie Gene's face.

Had they heard the strange scream, too? Or were they coming because they'd heard him trying to break down Susan's door?

He had no time to explain what he was doing or why he was doing it. For the same mysterious reason that was making him try to break down her door, his sense of urgency had just multiplied tenfold.

The third meeting of shoulder to door had the door splintering as it separated itself from the doorjamb. What was left of the door instantly slammed into the opposite wall as Duke ran in, bellowing Susan's name at the top of his lungs.

In response he heard that same muffled, strange scream, even more urgent this time than before.

It took him more than half a minute to realize what was going on, the lag due to the fact that it all looked so surreal, literally as if it had been lifted from some bad slasher movie.

Susan had silver tape wrapped around over half her body, sealing her to one of her kitchen chairs. There was blood on her, blood on the floor and a deranged-looking man wielding a knife which he nervously shifted back and forth, holding it to Susan's throat, then aiming it toward Duke to keep him at bay. The man continued to move the knife back and forth in jerky motions, as if he couldn't decide which he wanted to do more—kill Susan or kill Duke.

Duke wasn't about to give the man a chance to make up his mind.

With a guttural yell that was pure animal, Duke sailed through the air and threw himself against Susan's attacker, knocking the man to the floor. The assailant continued to clutch his knife. Duke saw the blood on it.

Susan's blood.

Sick to his stomach, he almost threw up.

And then a surge of adrenaline shot through him. Duke grabbed the man's wrist, forcing him to hold the knife aloft where, he hoped, the sharp blade couldn't do any harm.

Restraining Susan's attacker wasn't easy. The man turned out to be stronger than he looked, or maybe it was desperation that managed somehow to increase his physical strength. Duke didn't know, didn't have the time to try to analyze it and didn't care. All he knew was that he had to save Susan at any cost, even if it meant that he would wind up forfeiting his own life in exchange.

It was at that moment, with adrenaline racing wildly through his veins as he faced down a madman with a knife, that Duke realized that without Susan, he didn't have a life, or at least, not one that he believed was worth living.

204 *Colton by Marriage*

It was a hell of an awakening.

"Who the hell are you?" Duke bellowed as he continued to grapple with the man.

"I'm Hank McWilliams, the husband of the woman you killed," he replied angrily, stunning Duke.

McWilliams wrenched his hand free and slashed wildly at Duke's shoulder. He hit his target, piercing Duke's flesh and drawing blood. He also succeeded in enraging Duke further.

The fight for possession of the weapon was intense, but ultimately short if measured in minutes rather than damage. Disarming McWilliams amounted to Duke having to twist his arm back so hard that he wound up snapping one of the man's bones.

Sounding like a gutted animal, McWilliams's shrill scream filled the air.

Duke was aware of the sound of running feet somewhere behind him and cries of dismayed horror. Prepared for anything, he looked up to see Donald and Bonnie Gene charging into the house.

"I need rope to tie this bastard up," he yelled at Bonnie Gene, sucking in air. "Donald, call the sheriff. Tell my brother I caught the guy stalking Susan."

Grabbing a length of cord from one of the upper kitchen cabinets, Bonnie Gene ran back into the living room.

"Someone was stalking Susan?" she cried, alarmed.

Panting, Duke had already allowed Donald to take over holding McWilliams down. Donald had done it wordlessly by planting his considerable bulk on the man, who was lying facedown on the floor. Taking the rope from his wife, he tied McWilliams up as neatly as he'd tied any horizontally sliced tenderloin that had come across his work table.

Not waiting for an answer to her question, Bonnie Gene hurried over to her daughter, who was struggling to remain conscious.

Duke had already begun removing the duct tape from around her. Susan was trying not to whimper but every movement he made, however slight, brought salvos of pain with it.

"I'm sorry," Duke kept saying over and over again as he peeled away the duct tape. "I'm trying to be quick about it."

"It's okay," Susan breathed, struggling to pull air into her oxygen-depleted lungs.

"Oh, my poor baby," Bonnie Gene cried, feeling horribly helpless. A sense of torment echoed through her as she took in her daughter's wounds.

Standing back as Duke worked to remove the rest of the duct tape, Bonnie Gene quickly assessed the number of wounds that Susan had sustained. A cry of anguish ripped from her lips when she reached her total.

Bonnie Gene swung around and kicked McWilliams in the ribs six times, once for each stab wound that her daughter had suffered. As she kicked, Bonnie Gene heaped a number of curses on the man her husband had no idea she knew. Donald looked at her with renewed admiration.

"You're going to be okay, Susan, you're going to be okay. I don't think the bastard hit anything vital," Duke told Susan as he looked over her wounds.

He felt his gut twisting as he assessed each and every

one. As gently as he could, he picked Susan up in his arms and turned toward the door. He almost walked into Bonnie Gene, who was hovering next to him, trying hard not to look as frightened as she probably felt.

"I'm going to take Susan to the hospital," he told her mother.

Bonnie Gene bobbed her head up and down quickly, glad for the moment that someone had taken over.

"We'll use my car," she told him, digging into her pocket for her keys. "It's faster than your truck," she added when he looked at her quizzically.

"I'll get…blood…all over…it," Susan protested haltingly. The fifty-thousand-dollar car was her mother's pride and joy, her baby now that her children were all grown.

"Like I care," Bonnie Gene managed to get out, unshed tears all but strangling her. Getting out in front, she quickly led the way out of the house.

"Don't let him out of your sight until my brother gets here," Duke cautioned Donald just before he left the house with Susan.

"I'm not even going to let him out from under my butt," Donald assured him, raising his voice. "Just get my daughter to the hospital."

But he was talking to an empty doorway.

Looking back later, Duke had no idea how he survived the next few hours.

The moment Bonnie Gene drove them into the hospital's parking lot, he all but leaped out of the vehicle, holding an unconscious Susan in his arms, pressed against his chest. Silently willing her to be all right.

Terrified that she wasn't going to be.

A general surgeon was on call. One look at Susan and Dr. Masters had the nurses whisking her into the operating room to treat the multiple stab wounds on her torso. The surgeon tossed a couple of words in their general direction as he hurried off to get ready himself.

That left Duke and Bonnie Gene waiting in the hall as the minutes, which had flowed away so quickly earlier, now dragged themselves by in slow motion, one chained to another.

There was nothing to do but wait and wait. And then wait some more.

Duke wore a rut in the flat, neutral carpeting in the hallway directly outside the O.R. His brain swerved from one bad scenario to another, leaving him more and more agitated, pessimistic and progressively more devastated with every moment that went by.

Sometime during this suspended sentence in limbo, Donald arrived to ask after his youngest daughter and to tell them what had happened at the guest house after his wife and Duke had left. The sheriff had arrived soon after they drove off for the hospital, and Donald had quickly filled Wes in on what he knew, which wasn't much. After turning McWilliams over to the sheriff, Donald had sped to the hospital.

"She's a strong girl," Donald assured Duke, taking pity on the young man. "She takes after my side of the family."

Bonnie Gene looked up, leaving the dark corridors of her fears. Though she was trying to keep a positive outlook, it was still difficult not to give in to the fears that haunted every mother.

"Susan gets her strength from my side of the family," Bonnie Gene contradicted.

"Right now, she needs all the strength she can beg, borrow or steal from both sides," Duke told the pair impatiently. The last thing he was in the mood for was to listen to any kind of bickering.

Bonnie Gene rose, taking a deep, fortifying breath and doing her best to look cheerful, even as she struggled with the question of how this could have happened to her baby. And right under her nose, too.

She put her hand on Duke's shoulder, giving it a quick squeeze. "She'll pull through, Duke. Susan might not look it, but she's a fighter." Her eyes met Donald's for affirmation. "She always has been."

Duke made no response. He really didn't feel like talking. So, instead, he took a deep breath and just nodded, silently praying that Bonnie Gene was right.

With effort, he maintained rigid control over his mind, refusing to allow himself to think about what might have happened if he hadn't come when he had.

If he'd worked more slowly and arrived an hour later.

There was a definite pain radiating out from his heart. A pain, he was certain, he would have for the rest of his life if Susan didn't pull through.

"She didn't look very strong when they took her into the O.R." Until he heard his own voice, he wasn't even aware of saying the words out loud.

Bonnie Gene pressed her lips together, pushing back an unexpected sob.

"That's my Susan, soft on the outside, tough on the inside. You're not giving her enough credit," she told Duke. "But you'll learn."

The woman said that as if she believed that he and her daughter would be together for a long time, Duke noted. Bonnie Gene had more confidence in the future than he did, he thought sadly.

The next moment, the O.R. doors swung open, startling all three of them. It was hard to say who pounced on the surgeon first, Bonnie Gene, Donald or Duke.

But Duke was the first who made a verbal demand. "Well?"

Untying the top strings of his mask and letting it dangle about his neck, Dr. Masters offered the trio a triumphant, if somewhat weary smile.

"It went well. She's a tough one, luckily," he declared.

"I told you," Bonnie Gene said to Duke. She almost hit his shoulder exuberantly, stopping herself just in time, remembering that McWilliams had sliced him there and he'd had to have it treated and bandaged.

Duke wasn't listening to Bonnie Gene. His attention was completely focused on the surgeon. "Will she be all right?"

Masters looked a bit mystified as he continued filling them in. "Yes. Miraculously enough, none of her vital organs were hit. Don't know how that happened, but she is an extremely lucky young woman." He looked at the trio, glad to be the bearer of good news. "You can see her in a little while. She's resting comfortably right now, still asleep," he added. "A nurse will be out to get you once she's awake."

Duke didn't want to wait until Susan was awake. He just wanted to sit and look at her, to reassure himself that she was breathing. And that she would go on breathing. He slipped away from Susan's parents and went in search of her.

He slipped into Susan's room very quietly, easing the door closed behind him.

She did look as if she was sleeping, he thought. He fought the urge to reach out and touch her, to push a strand of hair away from her face and just let his fingertips trail along her cheek.

She was alive. Susan was alive. She'd come close to death today, but she was still here. Still alive. Still his.

He let out a long, deep breath that had all but clogged his lungs. He never wanted to have to go through anything like that again.

Seizing one of the two chairs in the room, he brought it over to her bed, sat down and proceeded to wait for Susan to wake up.

He didn't care how long it took, he just wanted to be there when she opened her eyes.

Chapter 16

Consciousness came slowly, by long, painfully disjointed degrees. Throughout the overly prolonged process, Susan felt strangely lightheaded, almost disembodied, as if she was floating through space without having her body weighing her down.

Was this what death felt like?

Was she dead?

She didn't think so, but the last thing she remembered was Duke carrying her to the car—her mother's car—and she was bleeding. Bleeding a lot and feeling weaker and weaker.

After that, everything was a blank.

Was heaven blank?

Struggling, Susan tried to push her eyelids up so that she could look around and find out where she was. But she felt as if her eyelids had been glued down. Not only that, but someone had put anvils on each of them for good measure. Otherwise, why couldn't she raise them at will?

She was determined to open her eyes.

Something told her that if she didn't open them, she was going to fade away until there was nothing left of her but dust. Dust that would be blown off to another universe.

She liked *this* universe.

This universe had her parents in it. And her siblings.

And Duke.

Duke.

Duke had saved her. Did that mean that he loved her? Whether he loved her or not, she didn't want to leave Duke, not ever.

With a noise that was half a grunt, half a whimper, she concentrated exclusively on pushing her eyelids up until she finally did it.

She could see.

And what she saw was Duke.

Duke was standing over her, looking worn and worried. More worried than she remembered ever seeing him. His left arm was in a sling, but he was holding her hand with his right hand.

He didn't believe in public displays of affection, she thought. But he was holding her hand. In a public place.

Was she dead?

"Duke?" she said hoarsely.

He'd never cried. Not once, in all his thirty-five years. Not when Damien was convicted of murder and they had taken him out of the courtroom in chains. Not even when that horse had thrown him when he was ten and had come damn near close to stomping him to death, only his father had jumped into the corral and dragged him to safety at the last minute, cursing his "brainless hide" all the way.

He hadn't cried then.

But he felt like crying now. Crying tears of relief to release the huge amount of tension that he felt throbbing all through him.

She was alive.

"Right here," he told Susan, his reply barely audible. Any louder and she'd be able to hear the tears in his throat.

"I know...I can...see...you," she answered, each word requiring a huge effort just to emerge. Her hand tightened urgently on his. "Charlene's...husband...tried to...kill...me."

"He won't hurt you any more," Duke swore. *Not even if I have to kill him with my bare hands,* he promised silently.

"He...didn't want to...hurt...me, he...wanted to... hurt...you," she told Duke, then rested for a second, the effort to talk temporarily draining her.

"Hurt me?" Duke echoed incredulously. Was she still a little muddled, reacting to the anesthetic? She'd been the one to receive all the blows, he thought angrily. Again he promised himself that if by some miracle, Hank McWilliams was ever released from prison, he was going to kill the man. Slowly and painfully, to make him pay for what he'd done to Susan. And even then it wouldn't be enough.

"Yes... By hurting...someone you...loved," she told

him. A weak smile creased her lips. "I…guess…he… wasn't…very…smart."

Duke realized what she was saying. That McWilliams had made a mistake. But the man hadn't. McWilliams had guessed correctly. "No, I guess he's smarter than he looks," he told her pointedly.

Susan's eyes widened. The words were still measured, but were now less labored coming out. "That…would mean…that…you—"

"Love you," he finished the sentence for her. And then he smiled. "Yes, it would. And yes, I do."

This had been the hardest thing he had ever had to say. But today had taught him that not saying this would have taken an even heavier toll on him. Because he would have carried the weight of this lost opportunity around with him for the rest of his life.

Susan passed her hand over her forehead. She was back to wondering if she had indeed died. At the very least, "I…must be…hallucinating."

He smiled. "No, you're not. I'll say it again. I love you."

It was a tad easier the second time, he thought. But not by much. If he was going to say it the way he felt it, it was going to take practice. Lots and lots of practice.

"Maybe I'm…not…hallucinating," she allowed slowly. "Maybe this…is a dream…and if it is…I just won't…let…myself…wake up." Because hearing Duke say he loved her made her supremely happy and ready to take on the whole world—in small increments. "So, if that's…the case…if I'm…asleep…then I don't…have to worry…about sounding…like an idiot…when I…tell you…that I…love you."

"You wouldn't sound like an idiot. You *don't* sound like an idiot," he assured her softly.

So this was how it felt.

Love.

Exciting and peaceful at the same time. Duke grinned to himself. Who knew?

"Ask her to marry you already." Bonnie Gene's disembodied voice ordered impatiently from the hallway. She'd gone to fetch them both coffee and arrived back in time for this exchange. She'd been waiting outside the door for the last ten minutes. "I can't stand outside this door much longer."

Duke laughed, shaking his head. These Kelleys were a hell of a lively bunch. They were going to take some getting used to. In a way, he had to admit he was looking forward to it.

"So don't stand outside the door any longer. Come on in, Bonnie Gene," he urged.

The next moment, Susan's mother, carrying two containers of coffee, one in each hand, eased the door open with her back and came into the room.

"The heat of the coffee was starting to come through the containers," she informed them with a sniff, putting both coffees down on the small table. "I felt like I was standing outside in the hall forever, waiting for you to get around to the important part."

"And what makes you think I was going to get around to the 'important part'?" he asked, wondering if he should be annoyed at the invasion of his privacy, or amused that the woman just assumed that everything was her business. He went with the latter.

Bonnie Gene waved her hand, dismissing his attempt to be vague.

"Oh, please." She rolled her eyes. "You risked getting yourself killed to save my daughter, then, your shoulder bleeding like a stuck pig, you picked her up in your arms and looked like you were ready to carry her all the way to the next town on foot. Besides—" Bonnie looked up into his face and patted his cheek "—one look into your eyes and anyone would know how you feel."

"I didn't," Susan protested, weakly coming to her hero's aid.

"That's because you're still a little out of your head, my darling. You're excused." Taking her container back into her hands, Bonnie Gene removed the lid, then looked up at Duke pointedly. "All right, so when's the wedding?"

"Mother!"

Susan had used up the last of her available breath to shout the name as if it were a recrimination. It was one thing to kid around. It was completely another to put Duke on the spot like this.

In addition to beginning to really hurt like hell, Susan was now also mortified. Didn't her mother take any pity on her?

"As soon as she's well enough to pick out a wedding dress," Duke replied quietly, answering Bonnie Gene's question.

"Mother, please, you can't just—" And then Susan's brain kicked in, echoing the words that Duke had just uttered. Stunned, Susan attempted to collect herself. She had to ask. "Duke, did you just say something about a wedding dress?"

"He did," Bonnie Gene gleefully answered the question before Duke could.

"Whose?" Susan all but whispered. They'd established that she wasn't dead. But maybe she had a concussion.

"Yours," Duke told her, beating Bonnie Gene to the punch this go-round. And then he looked at the older woman who seemed so bent on being involved in all the facets of their lives. "You *are* going to stay home when we go on our honeymoon, aren't you?"

Delighted, Bonnie Gene smiled from ear to ear. "I don't think you two need any help there."

Duke breathed a genuine sigh of relief. For a second, he'd had his doubts. "Good."

"Hey, wait a minute," Susan did her best to call out, feeling completely out of it and ignored. "Haven't you forgotten something?"

With effort, she pushed the button that raised the back of the bed, allowing her to assume the semblance of a sitting position.

Duke thought for a moment, stumped. And then it came to him. "Oh, right." Duke reached for her with his free arm, lowering his head to hers in order to kiss her.

Susan put her hand up in front of her mouth, blocking access. "No, wait. I mean you didn't ask me."

He pulled his head back, looking at her. "Ask you what?"

Either the man had an incredibly short attention span, or she was just not making herself clear. "To marry you."

"Oh."

He had taken her compliance for granted. It hadn't

occurred to him, after what they had just both been through, that she would turn him down. But maybe he was wrong. Maybe she didn't feel about him the way he did about her. Maybe this life-and-death experience had had a different effect on Susan, making her want to run into life full-bore and sample as much of it as she possibly could.

Because Bonnie Gene was looking at him expectantly, he went through the motions. Part of him was dreading the negative answer he might receive at the end. "Susan Kelley, will you marry me?"

"That's better." Pleased, Susan nodded her head in approval. "And yes, I'll marry you," she said with a deceptively casual tone, followed up with a weak grin. The grin grew in strength and size as she added, "Now you can kiss me."

"You going to give me orders all the time?" he asked, amused.

"No, I think you'll get the hang of all this soon enough." She glanced at Bonnie Gene. It was time for her mother to retreat. Far away. "Mother?"

"You want me to kiss him for you?" Bonnie Gene offered whimsically.

"Mother," Susan repeated more firmly this time, using all but the last of her strength.

With a laugh, Bonnie Gene raised her hands in total surrender. "I'm going, I'm going." But she stopped for a moment, growing a little serious. "Treat my daughter well, Duke Colton, or I will hunt you down and make you sorry you were ever born."

To his credit, he managed to keep a straight face. "Yes, ma'am."

Susan pointed toward the door. "Leave, Mother."

"Don't have to tell me twice," Bonnie Gene assured her, backing out of the room.

As the door closed behind her, a broadly grinning Bonnie Gene began to hum to herself.

One down, five to go.

* * * * *

COMING NEXT MONTH

Available July 27, 2010

ROMANTIC *SUSPENSE*

SRSCNM0710

REQUEST YOUR FREE BOOKS!

2 FREE NOVELS
PLUS
2 FREE GIFTS!

ᚦ Silhouette®
ROMANTIC
SUSPENSE

Sparked by Danger, Fueled by Passion.

SRS10R

Five hunky Texas single fathers—five stories from Cathy Gillen Thacker's LONE STAR DADS *miniseries. Here's an excerpt from the latest,* THE MOMMY PROPOSAL *from Harlequin American Romance.*

"I hear you work miracles," Nate Hutchinson drawled. Brooke Mitchell had just stepped into his lavishly appointed office in downtown Fort Worth, Texas.

"Sometimes, I do." Brooke smiled and took the sexy financier's hand in hers, shook it briefly.

"Good." Nate looked her straight in the eye. "Because I'm in need of a home makeover—fast. The son of an old friend is coming to live with me."

She was still tingling from the feel of his warm palm. "Temporarily or permanently?"

"If all goes according to plan, I'll adopt Landry by summer's end."

Brooke had heard the founder of Nate Hutchinson Financial Services was eligible, wealthy and generous to a fault. She hadn't known he was in the market for a family, but she supposed she shouldn't be surprised. But Brooke had figured a man as successful and handsome as Nate would want one the old-fashioned way. *Not that this was any of her business...*

"So what's the child like?" she asked crisply, trying not to think how the marine-blue of Nate's dress shirt deepened the hue of his eyes.

"I don't know." Nate took a seat behind his massive antique mahogany desk. He relaxed against the smooth leather of the chair. "I've never met him."

"Yet you've invited this kid to live with you permanently?"

"It's complicated. But I'm sure it's going to be fine."

Obviously Nate Hutchinson knew as little about teenage

boys as he did about decorating. But that wasn't her problem. Finding a way to do the assignment without getting the least bit emotionally involved was.

Find out how a young boy brings Nate and Brooke together in THE MOMMY PROPOSAL, coming August 2010 from Harlequin American Romance.